KT-233-372

This was too important to risk playing games with. Honesty couldn't hurt, surely?

Disarming...*charming* this man, even...might get him on side. *Her side.*

'The historical protection order,' she said. 'I've been expecting someone to come and want to see the house.'

'Ah...'

He was holding her gaze, and for a heartbeat Zanna had the impression he was about to tell her something of great significance. But then his gaze shifted and she could sense him changing his mind.

He nodded, as though confirming his decision. 'Yes,' he said, slowly. 'I *would* like to see the house.'

Should she show him? How dangerous would it be to be alone with this man? But what if he *did* hold the key to saving this place? How good would it be to have its safety assured by the time Maggie got home? She owed her beloved aunt so much, and a protection order would be a gift beyond price.

For both of them.

Zanna took a deep, steadying breath. And then she mirrored his nod. 'I'll have to lock up,' she told him. Moving to collect the key from behind the counter took her even closer to him, and she felt that odd curl of sensation deep within again. Stronger this time. That heady mix of desire laced with...danger.

She was playing with fire.

But, oh...the heat was delicious.

Dear Reader

A romance is all about its central characters and their journey, of course, but secondary characters are important too. Usually I find that they turn up as and when they're needed in a story, but this time it was a secondary character that inspired the story. And it isn't even a person!

I have to confess that I do have a passion for old houses. I think there's a good reason why they're called 'character' homes, because they *do* have personalities and you can certainly fall in love with them. My all-time favourite houses have turrets. There's a whisper of fairytale castles about them and a hint of possible magic.

While this special house that provided my inspiration has a part to play the real story is all about Zanna. And Nic. And, yes…there's a turret. And maybe a bit of magic too…

Happy reading! :-)

With love

Alison Roberts

IN HER RIVAL'S ARMS

BY

ALISON ROBERTS

First published in Great Britain 2014
by Mills & Boon, an imprint of Harlequin (UK) Limited,
Eton House, 18-24 Paradise Road, Richmond, Surrey, TW9 1SR

ISBN: 978-0-263-24300-0

Harlequin (UK) Limited's policy is to use papers that are natural, renewable and recyclable products and made from wood grown in sustainable forests. The logging and manufacturing processes conform to the legal environmental regulations of the country of origin.

Printed and bound in Great Britain
by CPI Antony Rowe, Chippenham, Wiltshire

Alison Roberts lives in Christchurch, New Zealand, and has written over sixty Mills & Boon® Medical Romances™.

As a qualified paramedic she has personal experience of the drama and emotion to be found in the world of medical professionals, and loves to weave stories with this rich background—especially when they can have a happy ending.

When Alison is not writing you'll find her indulging her passion for dancing or spending time with her friends (including Molly the dog) and her daughter Becky, who has grown up to become a brilliant artist. She also loves to travel, hates housework, and considers it a triumph when the flowers outnumber the weeds in her garden.

Recent titles by Alison Roberts:

THE MAVERICK MILLIONAIRE◊
FROM VENICE WITH LOVE‡
ALWAYS THE HERO††
NYC ANGELS: AN EXPLOSIVE REUNION~
ST PIRAN'S: THE WEDDING!†
MAYBE THIS CHRISTMAS…?
THE LEGENDARY PLAYBOY SURGEON**
FALLING FOR HER IMPOSSIBLE BOSS**
SYDNEY HARBOUR HOSPITAL: ZOE'S BABY*
THE HONOURABLE MAVERICK

‡*The Christmas Express!*
**Sydney Harbour Hospital*
†*St Piran's Hospital*
***Heartbreakers of St Patrick's Hospital*
~*NYC Angels*
††*Earthquake!*
◊*The Logan Twins*

This and other titles by Alison Roberts are available in eBook format from www.millsandboon.co.uk

DEDICATION

For the Maytoners, with love, in recognition of the magic you have all brought into my life. xxx

CHAPTER ONE

NO WAY WAS he a genuine customer.

Suzanna Zelensky had no need to call on any intuitive powers she might have inherited from her bloodline. Even the dark silhouette of this stranger, caused by the slant of late afternoon sunshine through the window behind him as he stepped further into her domain, radiated a palpable scepticism. He wanted nothing to do with anything this business represented. The impression wasn't all that uncommon in the gypsy shop Spellbound and it was almost always emanated by males, but they were invariably dragged in a by a female partner.

This man was alone and yet he moved with a determination that suggested he had a good reason for entering her world. Alarm bells rang with enough force to make the back of Zanna's neck prickle. Who was he and what did he want?

She had seen him well before he'd had the chance to see her. Had caught a clear glimpse of his face in that heartbeat of time from when he'd come through the door until he'd stepped forward into that shaft of light. Strong features with a shadowing to his jaw that accentuated uncompromising lines. A harsh but compelling face. This man wouldn't just stand out from a crowd.

He would render those around him virtually invisible. He was different. Beautiful…

Having other customers to attend to was fortunate. Zanna had time to think. A chance to consider the implications of this unusual visit and an opportunity to gather her emotional resources. She turned back to the teenage girls.

'You'll need a burner to use the essential oils as aromatherapy. We have a good range over here.' The heavy silver bangles Zanna was wearing gave the movement of her arm a distinctive, musical accompaniment.

She could feel him looking at her now. A predatory kind of appraisal that should have raised any hackles she possessed but instead, disturbingly, she could feel a very different kind of response. Her skin prickled as though every cell was being stirred. Coming alive.

'How do they work?' One of the girls was reaching for a burner.

'A small candle goes in the base.' Zanna risked a quick glance behind her, maybe because she had sensed she was no longer under scrutiny. Sure enough, the man was moving, staring at the objects on display. For a moment, Zanna stared blankly at the object in front of *her*. What had she been talking about?

'You put water in the bowl above it,' she managed, 'and sprinkle a few drops of your chosen oil on the water. As it heats, the scent is carried in the vapour.'

'What do these ones do?' A dark-haired girl picked up a tiny bottle.

'Those ones are designed to complement zodiac signs. They increase your personal powers.'

He was watching her again. Listening? Quite likely, given the increase in the strength of scepticism she could sense. Scathing enough to bring a rising flush of heat to her neck. Zanna had always loathed the fact that she blushed so easily and she particularly didn't appreciate it right now.

'I'm Sagittarius,' the blonde girl announced. 'Can I open the bottle and see what it smells like?'

'Sure.' Zanna moved away as the girls tested the oils. Despite being acutely aware of the movements of the stranger within the shop since he'd entered, she had made no direct acknowledgment of his presence. As far as he was concerned, he had been totally ignored, which was not a practice she would normally have employed with any potential customer. They couldn't afford to turn away business.

But this man wasn't a customer. The dismissive rake of his glance across shelves of ornate candle holders and chalices, stands of incense and display cases of Celtic jewellery, even before the flick of a finger against a hanging crystal prism that sent rainbow shards of light spinning across the ceiling, had confirmed that his mission did not include any desire to make a purchase.

He didn't look like someone who might have been drawn in for the refreshments available either. She could imagine him ordering a double-shot espresso to go, not lingering over herbal teas and organic cakes and cookies. Had he even noticed the blackboard menu as he'd raised his gaze? Had he been caught by the play of light on the ceiling from the prism or was he inspecting the intricate pattern of stained glass in the fanlights above the main windows?

He was moving away from her now, towards the selection of crystal stones in a basket near the window. He was tall. She knew he was over six feet in height because the circular feather and twine dreamcatchers suspended from the ceiling brushed the top of his head as he walked beneath them. His hair was black and sleek, the waves neatly groomed, with just enough length to curl over the collar of a well-worn black leather jacket. His jeans fitted like a glove and the footwear was interesting. Not shoes—boots of some kind. Casual clothing but worn in a way that gave it the aura of a uniform. Of being in command. A motorbike helmet was tucked under one arm.

Zanna could almost taste the testosterone in the air and it made her draw in a quick breath and take a mental step sideways.

Maybe those alarm bells had been ringing for a more intimate purpose. Perhaps her intuition had been overwhelmed by the raw sexual energy this man possessed. A subtle but determined shake of her head sent a lock of waist-length copper-coloured hair over one shoulder. She brushed the errant tress back calmly as she moved towards the stranger.

'Can I be of any assistance?'

Dominic Brabant almost dropped the stone he was weighing in a careless hand. He'd only seen the profile and then the back view of this woman when he'd entered the shop because she'd been busy with her customers. He'd had a good look at that back, mind you, while wrestling with the annoyance that two silly schoolgirls presented such an effective barrier to having a private conversation.

He could wait. He'd learned long ago that patience could be well rewarded.

Maybe he would go to one of the small wooden tables, screened by bookshelves, and order one of the teas described on the blackboard menu.

A ginger tea for its energising properties, perhaps?

No. He had more than enough energy. The motivation for being here in the first place had been validated in those few minutes he'd had to take, standing out there in the street, untangling the overload of memories and emotions. He could feel it fizzing in his veins and gaining strength with every passing minute. It had to happen. Fate had provided the opportunity and it felt like the inspiration had always been there, just waiting to be unleashed. The desire to succeed was more powerful than any that had preceded his achievements so far in life.

This was personal. Deeply personal.

He blew out a breath. Maybe a soothing chamomile tea might be the way to go. He couldn't afford to make this any more difficult than it had to be. And he wasn't even sure that this was the woman he needed to speak to. She might simply be a shop assistant who was paid to wear that ridiculous dark purple robe and improbable hair that had to be a wig. Nobody had real hair that could ripple down their back like newborn flames.

It was just part of the image. Like the flowing clothes and heavy silver bangles. The assumption that she was probably large and shapeless under that flowing fabric and that the hair under the wig was steely grey was blown away somewhat disconcertingly by the sound of her voice at close quarters.

The witch—if that was who she was, according to the information he'd been provided with—was young and the lilt in those few words created a ripple that was reminiscent of the silky fall of that wig.

He cleared his throat as he turned to meet her gaze. 'I'm just looking at the moment, thanks.'

A flash in her eyes let him know that she recognised

the ambiguity as he continued to look at her rather than what was for sale in the shop.

The sustained eye contact was unintentional. This wasn't the time to intimidate anyone—especially someone whose co-operation might be essential—but the proximity of the window gave this corner of the shop much more light than the rest of the candlelit interior. Enough light to see the copper-coloured rims around those dark, hazel eyes and the dusting of freckles on pale skin. And the hair was *real*. Or was it? Nic had to suppress an outrageous desire to reach out and touch the tendril caught on the wide sleeve of the robe. Just to check.

'Are you looking for something in particular?' Zanna held the eye contact with difficulty. The hint of a foreign accent in the stranger's deep voice was only faint but it was as intriguing, not to mention as sexy, as her earlier observations. The feeling of connection was more than a little disturbing. How could such an intensity be present so instantaneously?

And, yes…he was looking for something in particular.

Something he had promised when he'd been only six years old.

'When I'm big, Mama, I'll be rich. I'll buy that big house next door for you.'

Disturbingly, he could almost hear an echo of his mother's quiet laugh. Feel her arms holding him. The sadness that would always give her voice that extra note.

'Merci beaucoup, mon chéri. Ce sera merveilleux!'

'No.' The word came out more forcefully than he'd intended. He summoned at least the beginning of a smile. 'Nothing in particular.'

His eyes were dark. Almost black in this light. Inscrutable and unnerving. Resisting the instinct to look away was almost unbearable. The strength of will this man possessed was a solid force but she couldn't afford to lower her guard until she knew what his motives were in coming here.

He was bouncing the crystal in his palm. Zanna had the uncomfortable notion that it wasn't just the rock he was playing with. He had a purpose in coming in here. He wanted something from her. He wanted...*her*?

The ridiculous notion came from nowhere. Or was she picking up a well-hidden signal?

Whatever. It was strong enough to make her toes curl. To send a jolt right through her body, sparking and fizzing until it melted into a glow she could feel deep in her belly.

Desire? Surely not. That was a sensation she thought she might have lost for ever in the wake of the London fiasco with Simon. But what if it was? What if something she'd feared had died had just sprung to life again? She couldn't deny that the possibility was exhilarating.

It was also inappropriate. She knew nothing about this man and he could well represent a threat, both to herself and the only other person on the planet she had reason to cherish. Knowing she had to stay in control in the face of the power this stranger had the potential to wield over her physically was going to be a challenge.

And that was just as exhilarating as knowing she was still capable of experiencing desire. These last weeks, alone in both the shop and the house, had been lonely. Stifling, even.

The challenge was irresistible.

'You're holding a carnelian crystal.' She was pleased to find she could keep her tone pleasantly professional.

If she gave him something concrete to dismiss maybe he would reveal his true motive for being there. 'It's considered to be a highly evolved mineral healer that can aid tissue regeneration. It enhances attunement with the inner self and facilitates concentration.' She smiled politely. 'It opens the heart.'

'Really?' He couldn't help his sceptical tone. His own concentration had just been shot to pieces and he was still holding the stone.

Did some people really believe in magic?

Like they believed in love?

He released it to let it tumble back with its companions in the small wicker basket. He wasn't one of them.

'Excuse me.' The teenage girls had given up on the essential oils. 'What's in all those big jars?'

'They're herbs.'

It was hard to turn away from the man and that was a warning Zanna needed to listen to. A few moments to collect herself was a blessing but the task was made more difficult because the girls were staring at the man behind her now, their eyes wide enough to confirm her own impression of how different he was.

'Common ones like rosemary and basil,' she added, to distract them. 'And lots of unusual ones, like patchouli and mistletoe and quassia.'

Zanna never tired of looking at her aunt's collection of antique glass containers. They took pride of place on wide, dark shelves behind the counter, the eccentric shapes and ornate stoppers adding to the mysterious promise of the jars' contents. They had always been there. Part of her life ever since she'd arrived as a frightened young girl who had just lost both her parents. As grounding as being here, in the home she loved.

'They can be burned for aromatherapy or drunk as teas. They can also be used for spells.'

'Spells.' The girls nudged each other and giggled. 'That's what you need, Jen. A love spell.' They both sneaked another peek behind Zanna and Jen tossed her hair.

'Have a look at the book display,' Zanna suggested, unhappily aware that her tone was cool. 'There's some good spells in that small, blue book.'

'You have got to be kidding.'

The deep voice, unexpectedly close to her shoulder, startled Zanna and made her aware of another jolt of that delicious sensation. Cells that had already come alive caught alight. She could actually imagine tiny flames flickering over every inch of her skin.

'Got some eye of newt in one of those jars?'

Here it was. The first open evidence that this man was not a genuine customer. Zanna turned, her smile tight. 'No. We find that currants are a perfectly acceptable substitution these days.'

The giggles suggested the girls were oblivious to the tension that Zanna could feel steadily increasing. She cast a quick glance at the grandfather clock near the inner door of the shop. Only another ten minutes or so and she could close up and stop wasting her time with customers who either had no intention of buying anything or schoolgirls who couldn't afford to. At least the girls were enjoying themselves. The stranger wasn't. She could sense his irritation with the girls. Why? Was he waiting for them to leave? So he could be alone with her?

The flames flickered again but it was beyond the realms of possibility that the strength of the physical connection she could feel was being reciprocated. He wanted her for something, though… Of *course*…why hadn't she thought of that the moment she'd seen him come in, looking as though he had ownership of whatever—and *whoever*—was around him? As if he had the power to snap his fingers and change her world? To give her exactly what she wanted most.

Or to take it away.

Zanna stilled for a moment. Could he have come from the offices of the city council? They were as keen as the owner of the dilapidated apartment block next door that this property be sold and both the buildings destroyed in order to make a fresh development possible. There'd been veiled threats of the council having the power to force such a sale.

There was no sound of movement behind her either. Just a deep silence that somehow confirmed her suspicion and made her apprehensive.

Maybe the girls picked up on that. Or perhaps they'd seen Zanna look at the clock.

'Have you seen the time?' one of them gasped. 'We're going to be in *so* much trouble!'

They raced from the shop so fast the door banged and swung open again. Zanna moved to close it automatically and, without really thinking of why she might be doing it, she turned the sign on the door around to read 'Closed'.

She turned then. Slowly. Feeling like she was turning to face her fate.

And there he was. Relaxed enough to have one hip propped against the counter but watching her with a stillness about him that suggested intense concentration. Zanna felt a prickle of that energy reach her skin and she paused, mirroring his focus.

Something was about to happen.

And it was important.

His smile seemed relaxed, however. Wry, in fact, in combination with that raised eyebrow.

'You don't really believe in any of this stuff, do you?'

'What stuff in particular?' Zanna's heart picked up speed. If he was admitting his own lack of interest, maybe he was going to tell her why he was really here. 'There's rather a lot to choose from. Like aromatherapy, numerology, crystals, runes and palmistry. And the Tarot, of course.' Mischief made her lips curl. 'I would be happy to read your cards for you.'

He ignored the invitation. 'All of it.' His hand made a sweeping gesture. 'Magic.'

'Of course I believe in magic. I'm sure you do as well.'

The huff of sound was dismissive. *'Pas dans un million d'années.'*

The words were spoken softly enough that Zanna knew she had not been intended to hear them but the language was instantly recognisable. He was French, then. That explained the attractive accent and possibly that aura of control, too. She might not have understood the words but the tone was equally recognisable. Insulting, even. *Why* was he here—when he felt like this?

She'd had enough of this tension. Of not knowing.

'Are you from the council?'

As soon as the words left her mouth Zanna realised how absurd they were. It wasn't just because he was French that he had that quality of being in charge. A confidence so bone deep it could be cloaked in lazy charm. This man didn't work for anyone but himself. To suggest he might be a cog in a large, bureaucratic organisation was as much of an insult as dismissing everything that science was unable to prove. No wonder she could sense him gathering himself defensively.

'I beg your pardon?'

'You've come about the house?'

His hesitation spoke volumes. So did his eyes. Even if she had been close enough, those eyes were so dark already she might not have picked up the movement of his pupils but he couldn't disguise the involuntary flicker.

She'd hit the nail on the head and, for some reason, he was reluctant to admit it. Another possibility occurred to Zanna. He could be a specialist consultant of some kind and perhaps this was supposed to be an undercover inspection, in which case she might have been well advised to simply play along with the advantage of her suspicions. But this was too important to risk playing games. Honesty couldn't hurt, surely?

Disarming...*charming* this man, even, might get him on side. *Her* side.

'The historical protection order,' she said. 'I've been expecting someone to come and want to see the house.'

'Ah...' He was holding her gaze and, for a heartbeat, Zanna had the impression he was about to tell her something of great significance. But then his gaze shifted and she could sense him changing his mind. He nodded, as though confirming his decision. 'Yes,' he said, slowly. 'I *would* like to see the house.'

Should she show him? How dangerous would it be to be alone with this man? But what if he did hold the key to saving this place? How good would it be to have its safety assured by the time Maggie got home? She owed her beloved aunt so much and a protection order would be a gift beyond price.

For both of them.

Zanna took a deep, steadying breath. And then she mirrored his nod. 'I'll have to lock up,' she told him. Moving to collect the key from behind the counter took her even closer to him and she felt that odd curl of sensation deep within again. Stronger this time. That heady mix of desire laced with…danger.

She was playing with fire.

But, oh…the heat was delicious.

'I'm Zanna,' she heard herself saying. 'Zanna Zelenksy.'

'Dominic Brabant.' It was only good manners to extend his hand and his smile disguised the satisfaction of confirming that she was the person he'd been hoping to meet. 'Nic.'

'Pleased to meet you, Nic.'

The touch of her hand was as surprising as hearing her voice had been. That familiar *frisson* he noted would have been a warning in years gone by but Nic had learned to control it. To take the pleasure it could offer and escape before it became a prison.

Not that he'd expected to find it here. Any more than he'd expected this opportunity to appear. Fate was throwing more than one curveball in his direction at the moment. But how was he supposed to handle this one?

He watched as Zanna dipped her head, holding her hair out of the way, to blow out the numerous candles burning on the counter. With swift movements she divided and then braided the hair she held into a loose, thick rope that hung over her shoulder. Pulling a tasselled cord around her neck released the fastening of the purple robe. Skin-tight denim jeans appeared and then a bright orange cropped top that left a section of her belly exposed. There was a jewel dead centre. Copper coloured. It made him remember her extraordinary eyes. And as for her skin…

His gut tightened in a very pleasurable clench. The notion of her being a witch was too absurd. He was quite certain he would be unable to discover a single wart on that creamy skin.

Anywhere.

Mon Dieu… His body was telling him exactly how he would prefer to handle this and it didn't dent his confidence. It was a given that he would win in the end because he had never entertained the acceptance of failure since he'd been old enough to direct his own life, and this new project was too significant to modify.

Could what was happening here work in his favour?

Be patient, he reminded himself. He needed to go with the flow and see what other surprises fate might have in store for him.

The ripple of anticipation suggested that the reward would be well worth waiting for.

CHAPTER TWO

STONE GARGOYLES SAT on pedestals, guarding the steps that led to the shop's entrance. While Zanna fitted an old iron key into the lock and turned it, Nic took another stride or two onto the mossy pathway beneath massive trees.

Having already admitted his interest, he didn't have to stifle the urge to look up through the branches to get another look at the house. Zanna's distraction was fortunate because it gave him a few moments to deal with a fresh wave of the turbulent emotions that memories evoked.

It had to be his earliest-ever memory, running down a brick pathway just like this, summoned by the creak of the iron gate that announced his father's return home. Being caught in those big, work-roughened hands and flung skywards before being caught again. Terrifying but thrilling because it was a given that nothing bad could happen when Papa was there.

He could hear the faint echo of a small child's shriek of laughter that blended with the deep, joyous rumble of the adult.

Piercing happiness.

Nothing bad *had* happened while Papa had been there. Life had been so full of laughter. Of music. The sounds of happiness that had died when Papa had been snatched away from them.

The memory slipped away, screened by filters the years had provided. And he could help them on their way by focusing on the house and using his professional filter—an extensive knowledge of architecture and considerable experience in demolishing old buildings.

It really *was* astonishing, with the unusual angles to its bays and verandas that gave it the impression of a blunted pentagon. It was iced with ornate ironwork, intricately moulded bargeboards and modillions and, to top it all off, there was a turret, set like a church spire to one side of the main entrance, adding a third storey to the two large rooms with rounded bay windows.

A secret, circular room that begged to be explored.

Especially to a small boy who had gazed at it from over the fence.

The shaft of remembered longing was as shiny as that moment of happiness had been. The filters were like clouds, shifting just enough to allow a bright beam to shine through. Bright enough to burn.

The emotion behind this current project would be overwhelming if he let it surface. Not that his mother was here to see it happen but that only made it more important. This was going to be a memorial to the one woman he'd ever truly loved. To the man she'd loved with all her heart. To the family he'd had for such a heartbreakingly short breath of time.

He swallowed hard.

'It's amazing, isn't it?' Zanna had joined him on the path. 'The most amazing house in the world.'

A leaf drifted down from one of the trees and landed

on Nic's shoulder. Zanna resisted the urge to reach up brush it off.

'It's certainly unusual. Over a hundred years old. Queen Anne style.'

Had she been right in guessing that he was a specialist in old houses? 'How do you know that?' she asked. 'Are you an architect?'

'Used to be. Plus, I've done a lot of study. The style was taken up in the 1880s and stayed popular for a long time. The Marseilles tiles on the roof make it a bit later because they weren't introduced until about 1901.'

The brief eye contact as he glanced at her was enough to steal Zanna's breath for a moment. The connection felt weird but gave her hope. He knew about old houses. Would he fall in love with *her* house and help her fight to save it?

'I didn't know about the Queen Anne style until recently,' she confessed. 'I had to do some research to apply for the historical protection order. It's all about the fancy stuff, isn't it? The turret and shingles and things.'

It didn't matter if he didn't admit that consideration for protection was the reason he was here. Zanna was asking the question partly because she wanted him to keep talking. She loved his voice. It reflected the dark, chocolate quality of his eyes. And that faint accent was undeniably sexy.

'It was also known as free classical,' he told her. 'The turret *is* a bit of a signature. Like those dragon spikes on the roof ridges. It looks like it was designed by an architect with a strong love of fairy-tales.'

'Or magic?' Zanna suggested quietly.

He shook his head, dismissing the suggestion, but the huff of his breath was a softer sound than she might have expected. 'Typical of New Zealand to adopt a style and make it popular only after it was considered passé by the rest of the world.'

'So you're not a kiwi, then?'

'By birth I am. My mother was French. A musician. She came across a kiwi backpacker who'd gone to Paris to trace his own French ancestry. She found him sitting in a park, playing a guitar, and she said she fell in love with him the moment she heard his music.'

Why was he telling her this? Were memories coming at him so hard and fast they had to escape? No. Maybe it was because he'd had more time to process these ones. They'd been spinning and growing in his head and his heart for days. They'd inspired this whole project.

'She came back here to marry him and I was born the same year. He…died when I was five and I got taken back to France a year or so later.'

Turning points. When life had gone so wrong. He couldn't fix that, of course. But he could honour the time when it had been perfect. Not that he could share any of that with Zanna. Maybe he'd already said too much.

'I still have a home there,' he finished. 'But I also live in London.'

Zanna's eyes were wide. 'I've lived here since *I* was six. My parents got killed in a car accident and my aunt Magda adopted me. I've only recently come back, though. *I've* been in London for the last few years.'

The point of connection brought them instantly that little bit closer and Nic was aware of a curl of warmth but then, oddly, it became an emotional seesaw and he felt disappointed. So they'd been living in the same city, oblivious to the existence of each other? What a waste…

Another leaf drifted down. And then another. Zanna looked up, frowning.

'I'd better get some water onto these trees. It's odd. I didn't think the summer's been dry enough to distress them.'

'Maybe autumn's arriving early.'

'They're not deciduous. They're southern ratas. They don't flower very well more than once every few years but when they do, they're one of our most spectacular native trees. They have bright red, hairy sort of flowers—like the pohutukawa. The street was named after them. And the house. But they were here first and they're protected now, which is a good thing.'

'Why?'

'The trees are big enough to make it harder to develop the land—if it's ever sold.'

'You're thinking of selling?' Maybe this mission would end up being easier than expected. Done and dusted within a few days, even. Strange that the prospect gave him another pang of…what *was* that? Like knowing that he'd lived in the same city as Zanna without knowing about it. Not quite disappointment…more like regret?

Yet he knew perfectly well that the world was full of beautiful women and he'd never had trouble attracting his fair share of them. What was it about Zanna Zelenksy? Her striking colouring? Those eyes? The strong character?

She certainly wasn't feeling it. Her face stilled and he could see a flash of strong emotion darken her eyes.

'Not in my lifetime. This is my home. My refuge.'

Refuge? What did she need to run and hide from? Was there a streak of vulnerability in that strength? Yes…

maybe that was why his interest had been captured. But Zanna ignored his curious glance and began walking down the path.

'It's part of the city's heritage, too,' she flung over her shoulder. 'Only the council's too stupid to recognise it. They'd rather see it pulled down and have some horrible, modern skyscraper take its place.'

It wouldn't be a skyscraper.

It would be a beautiful, low building that echoed the curve of the river.

The Brabant Academy. A music school and performance centre, funded by the trust that would bring brilliant musicians together to nurture young talent. A serene setting but a place where dreams could be realised. A place of beautiful music. And hope for the future.

Nic followed her along the path. Heritage was often overrated, in his opinion. A smokescreen that could hide the truth that sometimes it was preferable to wipe out the past and put something new and beautiful in its place.

And this was one of those times. A final sweeping glance as he reached the steps leading to the main entrance of the house revealed the cracked weatherboards and faded shingles. Peeling paint and rust on the ironwork. Poverty and neglect were stamped into the fabric of this once grand residence and it struck deeply engrained notes in Nic's soul.

A new memory of his father surfaced.

'Why on earth would we want a grand old house that would take far too much money and time? We have everything we need right here, don't we?'

The tiny cottage *had* contained everything they'd needed. It had been home.

The shock of moving to the slums of Paris had been all the more distressing. The smell of dirt and disease and...death.

Yes. The hatred of poverty and neglect was well honed. Memories of the misery were powerful enough to smother memories of happier things so it was no surprise that they were peeking out from the clouds for the first time ever. Maybe he would welcome them in time but they were too disturbing for now. They touched things Nic had been sure were long dead and buried. They had the potential to rekindle a dream that had been effectively crushed with his mother's death—that one day he would again experience that feeling like no other.

The safety of home. Of family.

Zanna found she was holding her breath as she turned the brass knob and pushed open the solid kauri front door of her home.

First impressions mattered. Would he be blown away by the graceful curve of the wide staircase with its beautifully turned balustrade and the carved newel posts? Would he notice that the flower motif on the posts was repeated in the light switches and the brass plates around the doorknobs—even in the stained glass of the windows?

Maybe he'd be distracted by the clutter of Aunt Maggie's eccentric collections, like the antique stringed instruments on the walls above the timber panelling and the arrays of unusual hats, umbrellas and walking sticks crowding more than one stand on the polished wooden floorboards.

He certainly seemed a little taken aback as he stepped into the entranceway but perhaps that was due to the black shape moving towards them at some speed from out of the darkness of the hallway beneath the stairs.

Three pitch-black cats with glowing yellow eyes. Siblings that stayed so close they could appear like one mythical creature sometimes. She could feel the way Nic relaxed as the shape came close enough to reveal its components.

'Meet the M&Ms.'

'Sorry?'

Zanna scooped up one of the small, silky cats. 'This is Marmite. The others are Merlin and Mystic. We call them the M&Ms.'

'Oh…' He was looking down at his feet. Merlin, who was usually wary of strangers, was standing on his back feet, trying to reach his hand. He stretched out his fingers and the cat seemed to grow taller as he pushed his head against them.

Artistic fingers, Zanna noted, with their long shape that narrowed gradually to rounded tips. If Aunt Maggie were here, she'd say that this man was likely to be imaginative, impulsive and unconventional. That he'd prefer an occupation that gave him a sense of satisfaction even if it was poorly paid.

He'd said he used to be an architect. What did he do now? Consulting work with organisations like the historical protection society? It certainly seemed to fit.

Those artistic fingers were cupped now, shaping the cat's body as they moved from its head to the tip of the long tail. Merlin emitted a sound of pleasure and Zanna had to bury her face in Marmite's fur to stifle what could have been a tiny whimper of her own. She could almost *feel* what that caress would be like.

It was Mystic that started the yowling.

'They're hungry,' Zanna said. 'If I don't feed them, they'll be a nuisance, so would you mind if we start the tour in the kitchen?'

'Not at all.'

She led him into the hallway—shadowy thanks to the obstructed light and the dark timber panelling on the walls. What saved it from being dingy was the large painting. A row of sunflowers that were vivid enough to cast an impression of muted sunshine that bathed the darkest point.

She knew that Nic had stopped in his tracks the moment he saw it. Zanna stopped, too, but not physically. Something inside her went very, very still. Holding its breath.

It doesn't matter what he thinks. What anybody else thinks...

The involuntary grunt of sound expressed surprise. Appreciation. Admiration, even?

Okay. So it *did* matter. Zanna could feel a sweet shaft of light piercing what had become a dark place in her soul. Not that she could thank him for the gift. It was far too private. Too precious.

Opening the door to the sun-filled, farmhouse-style kitchen—her favourite part of the house—accentuated the new pleasure. The knowledge that Nic was right behind her added a dimension that somehow made it feel more real. Genuine. Even if nothing else came of this encounter, it had been worth inviting this stranger into her world.

The surprise of the stunning painting had only been a taste of what was to come. Nic had to stop again as he entered the huge kitchen space, blinking as he turned his head slowly to take it all in. It should be a nightmare scene to someone who preferred sleek, modern lines and an absence of clutter. It was only a matter of time before he experienced that inner shudder of distaste but at least he knew it was coming. He would be able to hide it.

Cast-iron kettles covered the top of an old coal range and the collection of ancient kitchen utensils hanging from an original drying rack would not have been out of place in a pioneer museum. The kauri dining table and chairs, hutch dresser and sideboard were also museum pieces but the atmosphere was unlike any such place Nic had ever been in. Splashes of vivid colour from bowls of fruit and vegetables, unusual ornaments and jugs stuffed with flowers made the kitchen come alive.

The shudder simply wasn't happening. Instead, to his puzzlement, Nic found himself relaxing. Somehow, the overall effect was of an amazingly warm and welcome place to be. It felt like a place for…a family?

Abandoning his helmet on the floor, he sank onto a chair at one end of the long table as Zanna busied herself opening a can and spooning cat food into three bowls. When she crouched down, her jeans clung to the delicious curve of her bottom and the gap between the waistband and the hem of her orange top widened, giving him a view of a smooth back, interrupted only by the muted corrugations of her spine. He could imagine trailing his fingers gently over those bumps and then spreading them to encompass the curve of her hip.

Oh…*Mon Dieu…* The powerful surge of attraction coming in the wake of those other bursts of conflicting and disturbing emotions was doing his head in. He needed distraction. Fast.

Maybe that curious object wrapped in black velvet on

the table, lying beside a wrought-iron candelabra, would do the trick. Lifting the careful folds of the fabric, Nic found himself looking at an oversized pack of cards.

Witchy sort of cards.

The shaft of desire he was grappling with morphed into a vague disquiet. It was very rare to feel even slightly out of his depth but it was happening now. There was an atmosphere of mystery here. Of eccentricity that had an undercurrent of serenity that had to come from someone who knew exactly who they were. Or some-*thing*, perhaps, because he couldn't be sure whether the vibe was coming from Zanna or the house.

Weird…

'We keep them wrapped in black.' Zanna's voice was soft. And close. Nic looked up to see she had a pair of wine glasses dangling by their stems in one hand and a bottle in the other. She held it up in invitation and he nodded.

'Sure. Why not?'

The wine was red. Blood red. His disquiet kicked up a notch.

'Why?' he asked.

'It just seemed like a good idea.' Zanna wasn't meeting his eyes. 'A glass of wine is a nice way to wind down. We could go into the garden, if you like.'

He followed the direction of her gaze. French doors provided a glimpse of a bricked courtyard between the kitchen and a tangle of garden. An intimate kind of space.

'I'm fine here.' Nic cleared his throat. 'I meant why do you wrap those cards in black?'

'It's a neutral colour that keeps outside energy away.' Zanna had filled her own glass and she sat down at right angles to Nic.

'It's black magic, right? Witchcraft?'

The flash in those extraordinary eyes was enough to make Nic feel unaccountably apologetic.

'I don't believe in witchcraft,' Zanna said, her voice tight. 'And calling any of this black magic is an insult to my aunt. Her family can trace its roots back to the sixteenth century. They travelled around and made their living by things like fortune-telling. Aunt Maggie has a very strong affinity with her heritage. I've grown up with it and I love Maggie enough to respect it. I see it as another dimension—one that adds some colour and imagination to life and can help people cope with the hard stuff.' She closed her eyes and sighed. 'Sorry…I get a bit defensive. We've had people try and twist things into something they're not and then use it against her. Against us.'

Nic said nothing. He had a feeling he knew who those people might be. But they were out of the picture now. He was the one who got to decide how things would be handled from now on. Except that he had no idea. Yet. He stared at the cards.

'I've always thought of it as a load of rubbish,' he admitted. 'The fortune-telling, that is.'

'Depends on how you look at it.' Zanna reached out and touched the pack of cards with her fingertips. 'It's about symbols. They demand an active response. You have to think about how you really feel and trying to relate to an unexpected symbol like the picture on a card can make you consider a totally new dimension to a problem. I like to think of them as a tool for self-knowledge. A way of centring oneself, perhaps.'

'Seeing the future?' He couldn't help the note of derision but she didn't seem to take offence.

'I don't believe the future can be seen…but I don't believe things are necessarily fated to happen either. There are choices to be made that can radically alter the direction you take in life. Big choices. Little choices. So many that you don't even notice a lot of them but it pays to be aware. Some people think they have no control and they blame others when things go wrong. If you've made an active choice and things go wrong, you can learn from that experience and it's less likely to happen again.'

Like falling in love with the wrong person…

Inviting a complete stranger into your home…

'If you don't believe the future can be seen, how can you tell a fortune and say something's going to happen? Like a new job or overseas travel or…' he snorted softly '…meeting a tall, dark, handsome stranger?'

Was that a reference to himself? Was he *flirting* with her? Zanna knew the rush of heat would be showing in her cheeks. Did he know how good looking he was? Probably. Nobody could be out there looking like that in a world full of women and not find it incredibly easy to get whatever he wanted. Maybe toying was a better word, then. It made her remember the way he'd been looking at her when he'd been playing with that crystal in the shop. It made her remember the way he'd made her feel. That reawakening of desire.

How far could that go?

How far did she want it to go?

'Okay…' She avoided meeting his eyes. 'First off, I'd probably say that there was an opportunity of a new job or travel or something. You might not have been thinking about it but the idea would be planted and you'd be more open to new ideas because of that suggestion. You might recognise an opportunity and then you'd have a choice. Something would change. You'd either take that opportunity or be more content to stay where you were.'

'Do you tell your own fortune?'

She smiled. 'Occasionally. If I have a problem I want to think through. I prefer to have Aunt Maggie read my cards, though. It's great fun and the best way I know to have a really meaningful conversation. That's how this whole business started. Way back, before my time here, but I've had plenty of people tell me about it. They came to have their cards read and Maggie became a magnet for anyone with a problem. And she's such a warm and loving person she would offer them tea and cakes at the same time and it all just grew into a way she could make her living.'

She took a sip of her wine and Nic couldn't look away. He watched her bottom lip touch the glass and the way her throat rippled as she swallowed. He picked up his own glass to find it contained a surprisingly good red wine.

'Back then,' Zanna continued, 'before the city centre spread and the houses gave way to office blocks and hotels, there were streets and streets of cottages. Houses that had big gardens with lots of fruit trees. People kept chickens. Mr Briggs down the road even kept a goat. So many people. This was the big house but everyone was welcome. They all adored Maggie and this place was like a community centre. I remember it being like that when I was young.'

'But the houses have gone. There's no community now.' Okay, it was sad but things changed. Progress happened.

'Some of the people still come back and talk about the old days. They can't believe that the house and Maggie are just the same as ever and they love sharing the memories. She always promises she'll still be here the next time they come.'

She wasn't here now. If she was, Nic might have been tempted to ask to have his cards read so that he could see if she was as amazing as Zanna made her sound. Had she really helped solve problems for so many people?

'Can you read the cards?'

Her eyes widened. Surprise or shock? 'I've grown up with them…yes… I'm not as good as Maggie but I can certainly read them.'

'Would you read them for me?'

The hesitation was obvious. 'Are you sure you want me to?'

So that they could have a really meaningful conversation? So that he could sit here a while longer and put off thinking about why he was really here? Maybe even find a solution to his own problem?

Nic held her gaze. Long enough for a silent message that had nothing to do with fortune-telling. He wanted more than his cards read and that want was getting stronger by the minute.

'Yeah…' His voice was husky. 'I'm sure.'

CHAPTER THREE

HE HAD NO IDEA, did he, how much could be revealed in a reading? He was drinking his wine, leaning back in his chair and watching curiously as Zanna went through the ritual of lighting the five fat candles on the arms of the candelabra and opening a drawer to extract a tiny bottle of lavender oil that she sprinkled on the black velvet square.

'To cleanse the space,' she explained.

'Right...' The corner of his mouth quirked but his gaze had enough heat that she could only handle the briefest contact.

Was it what she was doing that had captured his attention so intently or was he watching *her*? Adding the impression to wondering what she was about to find out about *him* made her feel oddly nervous. She needed another mouthful of her wine.

'The first thing I need to do is pick a card to represent you as the significator.'

'The what?'

'Significator. The querent. The seeker of knowledge.' This was good. She could hide her nerves by doing something she knew she was good at. She spread the cards, face up, in front of her. The sound Nic made was incredulous.

'But they're beautiful… They look like artwork reproductions.'

'This set is based on one of the oldest known packs. Tarot cards have been around for five hundred years. The first known cards were painted in Italy during the Renaissance. Back around the second half of the fifteenth century.'

Was he impressed with her knowledge? Why did she *want* him to be? Zanna glanced up but Nic was staring at the cards. Many pictures depicted people and each card had a title.

'I don't like that one,' he muttered. 'I hope Death isn't going to appear in my line up.'

'The meaning isn't necessarily literal. The death card means that something must come to an end. Whether or not it's painful depends on the person's capacity to accept and recognise the necessity for that ending.' The words came easily because they'd been learned many years ago. 'Sometimes you have to let go of an old life in order to take the opportunity of a new and more fulfilling one.'

'That's very true.' Yes, he was impressed. 'Something I've always lived by, in fact.' There was a question in his eyes now. Or was it an accusation? 'Do *you*?'

Zanna blinked. This wasn't supposed to be about her. She retreated into card lore as she looked away. 'The cards are designed to portray a story. Kind of the rites of passage of an archetypal journey through life. Everybody faces the same sorts of challenges and problems—the same as they did five hundred years ago. People don't change and it's often a surprise to find how similar we are to those around us. Every situation is different but the challenges can be the same.'

'You don't really believe you can predict the future, do you?'

This time, Zanna was able to hold his gaze. 'I believe that particular choices and situations have led to where one is in life and the response to that position presents future choices and situations. Understanding why and how some things have happened is the best way to cast a more conscious influence on the future.' She gave herself a mental shake. 'Are you over forty years of age?'

That made *him* blink. 'Do I *look* like I'm over forty?'

A bubble of laughter escaped. 'You could be a well-preserved specimen. How old *are* you?'

'Thirty six. How old are *you*?'

'That's not the least bit relevant. You're the one I need to find a card for.'

'Hey…I answered *your* question.' There was an unguarded tone in his voice. A peep at a small boy having a playground conversation perhaps. It gave her a soft buzz of something warm.

'I'm twenty-eight,' she relented. 'Oh, yes…This is definitely you.' She picked up the card. 'The King of Pentacles.'

'Why?'

'He represents a strong, successful individual with a gift of manifesting creative ideas in the world. He also represents status and worldly achievement and has the Midas touch.'

He looked taken aback. Did he think that wearing well-worn leather and jeans would disguise his obvious lack of any serious financial hardship? That jacket had been expertly tailored to fit so well and the nails on the ends of those artistic fingers were beautifully manicured. His casual appreciation of the special wine she had chosen had been another giveaway. She placed the chosen card on the centre of the black cloth. Then she scooped up the rest of the pack and began shuffling the cards.

'That's a lot of cards.'

'Seventy-eight.' Zanna nodded. 'The major Arcana that is the depiction of the journey and then the minor Arcana. Four suits of Cups, Wands, Swords and Pentacles. They represent elements and experiences.' She spread the cards in a fan shape in front of Nic, facing down this time. 'Formulate your question or think about a problem you want clarified,' she invited. 'You don't have to tell me what it is. Then choose ten cards and hand them to me in the order selected.'

She placed the cards in set positions in the form of a Celtic cross. 'This card over yours is the first one we look at. It's the covering card. Where you are at the moment and the influences affecting you.' She turned it over. 'Hmm...interesting.'

He was sitting very still. He might think this was a load of rubbish but he was unable to stop himself buying into it.

'Why?'

'Page of Wands. It suggests that it's time to discover a new potential. Also suggests restlessness at work. Something's not going the way you want it to.' She touched the card at right angles to the one she'd just read. 'This is the crossing card. It describes what is generating conflict and obstruction at the moment.' She turned the card face up.

The oath Nic muttered was in French but needed no translation.

'You're taking the pictures too literally,' she told him.

'The Hanged Man is a symbol. It suggests that a sacrifice of some sort might be needed. Maybe there's something that would be difficult to give up but it needs to go because it's blocking progress.'

He was giving her that odd look again. As though he was including *her* in whatever thought processes were going on.

'This is the crowning card,' she continued. 'It represents an aim or ideal that is not yet actual.'

'The future?'

'Potentially.'

'What's the Queen of Wands?'

Should she tell Nic that the Queen of Wands was the card that had always been picked as the significator for her own readings?

'She's industrious, versatile, strong-willed and talented.' Zanna kept her eyes firmly on the card. 'She's also self-contained and stable. She holds her great strength and energy within, devoting them to the few things to which she chooses to give her heart.'

The moment's silence was enough to make her realise that she didn't need to tell Nic about her own relationship to this particular card. He was joining the dots all by himself.

'It may not mean a person, as such,' she added. 'It could mean that it's time to start developing her qualities yourself. Things like warmth and loyalty and being able to sustain a creative vision.'

He wasn't buying that. He'd made his mind up, hadn't he, and she could sense his immovability when that happened.

The card depicting the immediate future suggested a dilemma to be faced with either choice leading to trouble and the card representing the kind of response that Nic could expect from others was one of her favourites—the Lovers.

Nic clearly approved of it, too. 'Now, why didn't that one show up for my immediate future?' he murmured. 'That would have been something to look forward to.'

The tone of his voice held a seductive note that rippled through every cell in Zanna's body like a powerful drug. She hadn't felt this alive for so long.

Maybe she never had.

Had this man come into her life to teach her to feel things she didn't know she was capable of feeling?

What would she do if he touched her with the kind of intent that tone promised?

Could she resist? Would she even try?

Maybe not. Zanna did her best to quell the curl of sensation deep in her belly. The anticipation. 'You're being too literal again. This card is the view of others. It could be that you're doing something to make them think as they do.'

She could sense his discomfort and it was disturbing.

He may not be who he seems to be. Take care...

She knew he might be dangerous. It was reckless to be taking pleasure from his company. From this anticipation of what might be going to happen, but maybe that was what was making this such a thrill. Adding something wild and even more exciting to this chemical attraction.

It was an effort to keep her voice even. 'This particular card might mean that you have to make a choice and it probably concerns love. It might be choosing between love and a career or creative activity. Or it could be that you're involved in a triangle of some sort. Or that someone's trying to get you to marry in a hurry.'

He was shaking his head now. 'I never have to choose between love and my career. I've never even thought about marriage and I avoid triangles at all costs.'

He walked alone, then? He was unattached?

The thought should have made him seem more attractive but something didn't feel right.

Zanna read a few more of the cards before she realised what was nagging at the back of her mind. It was too much of a coincidence that she felt so involved with every interpretation he was making. For whatever reason, Nic had included *her* in the question or problem he had brought to this reading.

Why?

'This card represents your hopes and fears.'

'The Fool? Who isn't afraid of making a fool of themselves?'

'The fear might apply to the fact that a risk of some kind is required. It suggests that a new chapter of your life might be about to begin but it needs a willingness to take a leap into the unknown. It fits with a lot of other cards here.'

'What's the last one?'

'That position is the final outcome. It should give you some clues to answer the question you brought into the reading.' Her own heart picked up speed as she turned it over. 'Oh…'

The tension was palpable. Nic didn't have to say anything to demand an explanation.

'The Ace of Swords means a new beginning,' she told him quietly. 'But one that comes out of a struggle or conflict.'

He drained his glass of wine. It was all rubbish. So why did it feel so personal? It was obvious that Zanna was part of his immediate future. That it was going to be a struggle to get what he wanted. But did she really need to be sacrificed?

The thought was disturbing. She was part of this place and it felt like a home. A kind of portal to those memories buried so far back in his own story. Nic looked away from the table, his gaze downcast. It was the first time he'd noticed the floor of this space. A background of grey tiling that resembled flagstones had been inset with mosaic details. Starburst designs made up of tiny fragments of colour that dotted the floor at pleasingly irregular intervals.

'It's not original, is it?' he queried. 'The floor?'

'Depends what you mean by original.' Zanna was refilling his glass. 'The old floorboards became unsafe because they were rotten. Maggie and I have always considered our creative efforts pretty original, though.'

'You made this floor?'

'Yes.' She topped up her own glass. 'Took ages but we loved doing it. In fact, we loved it so much we did flagstones for the garden, too. And a birdbath.'

Nic shook his head. Extraordinary.

'Maybe it's something to do with gypsy blood. Making do with what you find lying around. We dug up so much old broken china around here that it seemed a shame not to do something with it so we broke it up a bit more and used it for mosaic work.'

'Taking an opportunity, huh? Dealing with a problem.'

'Yes.' She was smiling at him as if he'd understood something she'd been trying to teach. The sense of approval made him feel absurdly pleased with himself.

'So you really do come from a gypsy bloodline?'

'Absolutely. It's only a few generations ago that my

family on my father's side was travelling. Maggie was my dad's older sister. My great-grandfather was born in a caravan.'

'Where does the name Zelensky come from?'

'Eastern Europe. Probably Romania. That's where my aunt Maggie's gone now. She was desperate to find out more about her family before she's too old to travel.'

The smile curled far enough to create a dimple. 'What's funny?' Nic asked.

'Just that Maggie's got more energy and enthusiasm than most people half her age have. She's the most amazing woman I've ever known and I never fail to feel enormously grateful that she was there to rescue me when I got orphaned.'

Suddenly Nic wanted to change the subject but he wasn't sure why. Maybe he didn't want to be reminded that she was vulnerable. That she'd been a frightened child. That this place was her home. Her *refuge*. Because it would give her an advantage in the conflict he knew was coming?

That was weird in itself. Nic didn't let emotions sway business decisions.

This was hardly a business decision, though, was it? It couldn't be more different from the luxury resorts he'd become known for designing and developing in recent years. And the impulsive decision to buy into Rata Avenue had unleashed so many personal memories. This had nothing to do with business, in fact. This was deeply personal. A step back in time to where he'd spent the most vulnerable years of his own life.

Was that why this house felt so much like home?

He cast another glance around the kitchen. No, this was nothing like the fragments of memory he still had.

The kitchen in the cottage had been tiny and dark and it had taken a huge effort from Maman to keep it sparkling clean. There was something about this space that tugged hard at those memories, however. Some of those old utensils, perhaps—like the metal sieve that had holes in the shape of flowers? He dropped his gaze to the floor. To the fragments of the old china embedded in the tiles.

Blue and white were prominent but many had small flowers on them. Like that one, with a dusty pink rose. He almost didn't recognise his own voice when he spoke.

'Where did you say you got all the china?'

'We dug it up. Some of it was in our own garden but most came from next door where the park is now. There was a cottage there that was even older than this place. The council acquired the land and demolished the cottage before I came here but it was a long time before the site was cleaned up so it was like a playground for me. I knew I wasn't allowed to go too close to the river but once I started finding the pretty pieces of broken china, I didn't want to. It was like a treasure hunt I could keep going back to. I think that was where my love of flowers came from.'

But Nic wasn't listening to her words. He wasn't even thinking of how musical that lilt in her voice was. He was thinking of a china cup that had pink rosebuds on it and a gold handle. He could see his mother's hands cradling it—the way she had when she'd become lost in her sadness. He could see the look in her eyes above the gold rim of the cup that matched the handle. He could feel the sensation of being so lost. Not knowing what to do to make her smile again. To bring back the laughter and the music.

'When I'm big, Mama, I'll be rich. I'll buy that big house next door for you.'

How could grief be so sharp when it had been totally buried for so many years?

Maybe it wasn't Zanna's vulnerability he needed to worry about at all. It was his own.

The pain was timely. He was here for a reason—to honour his parents—and he couldn't let anyone else dilute that resolution. No matter how beautiful they were.

'I should go.' He glanced at his watch. How on earth had so much time passed? 'It's getting late.'

'But didn't you want to see the house?' There was a faint note of alarm in Zanna's voice. 'There's still time before it gets dark.'

'Another time perhaps.' Except the words didn't quite leave his mouth because Nic made the mistake of looking up again.

The sun was much lower now and the light in the room had changed, becoming softer and warmer. Shards of colour caught in his peripheral vision as the light came through stained-glass panels and bounced off cut crystals that were hanging on silver wires.

It made that amazing colour of Zanna's hair even more like flames. Glowing and so alive—like her eyes and skin, and that intriguing personality.

There was no point in seeing the rest of the house but he didn't want to leave just yet. He might not get another time with her like this. Before she knew who he was or what he wanted. And being with her—here—might be the only way to get more of those poignant glimpses into his own past. As painful as they were, they were also treasure. Forgotten jewels.

Was it wrong to want more?

Quite possibly, but—heaven help him—he couldn't resist.

'Sure,' he heard himself saying instead. 'Why not?'

Maybe it hadn't been such a good idea to give Nic a tour of the house.

It might have been better to let him wander around by himself. But how could she have known that he would pick out the features she loved most herself? That the feeling of connection would gain power with every passing room?

He commented on the graceful proportions of the huge downstairs rooms, the ornately carved fireplaces and the beautiful lead-light work of the stained-glass fanlights. He knew more than she did about old houses, too.

'Those ceiling roses were more than a decorative feature.' With his head tilted back to inspect the central light surround, the skin on his neck looked soft and vulnerable. Zanna could imagine all too easily how soft it would feel to her fingers. Or her lips…

'They're actually ventilators. Those gaps in the plasterwork were designed to let out hot air.'

'Useful.' Her murmur earned her a glance accentuated by a quirked eyebrow. Could he feel the heat coming from her body?

No. It definitely hadn't been such a good idea to do this. Zanna froze for a moment at the bottom of the staircase. The rooms on the next level were far more personal. What would he say when he saw more of her handiwork? Could it take away that sweet pleasure that his reaction to the sunflower painting had given her?

He hadn't stopped moving when she did so his body

came within a hair's breadth of bumping into hers. Her forward movement was an instinctive defence against such a powerful force and there was only one way to go.

Up the stairs.

Maggie's room was safe enough. So were the spare bedrooms but the bathroom was next and she stood back to let Nic enter the room alone. Folding her arms around her body was an unconscious movement that was both a comfort and a defence.

So far, the features of this house had been expected. Period features that were valuable in their own right. Things that could be salvaged and recycled so they wouldn't be lost and he wouldn't need to feel guilty about their destruction.

But this…

Nic was speechless.

The fittings were in keeping with the house. The claw-foot bath, the pedestal hand basin and the ceramic toilet bowl and cistern with its chain flush, but everything had been painted with trails of ivy. The tiny leaves on the painted vines crept over the white tiled walls from the arched window, making it appear as though the growth had come naturally from outside the house. The floor was also tiled in white but there were small diamond-shaped insets in the same shade of green as the ivy. The interior of the antique bathtub was also painted the same dark green.

'C'est si spécial…'

Reverting to the language of his heart only happened when something touched him deeply but he didn't translate the phrase as he walked back past Zanna. She didn't move so he kept going towards the last door that opened off this hallway.

Directly over the shop, this room shared the feature of a large bay window but here it had been inset with a window seat that followed the semi-circular line. A brass bed, probably as old as the house, had a central position and the colours in the patchwork quilt echoed those of the tiles in the nearby fireplace.

The walls were lined with tongue-and-groove timber that had been painted the palest shade of green. Dotted at random intervals, but no more than a few centimetres apart, were reproductions of flowerheads. Every imaginable flower could be found somewhere on these wooden walls. From large roses and lilies to pansies and daisies—right down to the tiniest forget-me-nots.

'The hours this must have taken…' Nic murmured aloud. 'It must have cost a fortune.'

'It was good practice.'

Startled, Nic turned to find he wasn't alone in the room any longer. That feeling he'd had earlier of being potentially out of his depth had nothing on the way the ground had just shifted beneath him.

'*You* painted these?'

The shrug was almost imperceptible but the modesty was appealing. 'Maggie gave me an encyclopaedia of flowers for my twelfth birthday. I added one almost every day for years.'

'And the ivy in the bathroom?'

'That was a wet May school holiday.' Another tiny shrug came with the hint of a smile. 'Maggie said it would keep me out of mischief.'

He stared at her. 'Do you know how extraordinary you are, Zanna Zelensky? How *talented*?'

She simply stared back at him. As though he'd said something wrong and she was trying to decide what to do about it. The moment stretched but Nic couldn't break the silence. The air hummed with a curious tension but he had no clue as to what might have caused it.

Finally, she spoke.

'There's one room you haven't seen yet.'

His nod was solemn. His mouth felt dry and he had to lick his lips.

The turret. The one room he'd wanted to see inside for as long as he could remember. The child buried deep inside was about to have his dearest wish granted. But… what if it was a disappointment? If it was nothing more than, say, a storage area?

He forced his feet to start moving. To follow Zanna up the narrow, spiral staircase that led to the secret room beneath the witch's hat of the turret. If it was less than he hoped for, he'd cope. He had with every other childish hope and dream that had been crushed, hadn't he?

Opening the small door at the top of the stairs, Zanna walked ahead of him. She said nothing. She didn't even turn around as she walked over to one of the arched windows and stared out as if she was giving Nic some privacy.

And maybe he needed it.

Despite the now rapidly fading day, the light was still good in here thanks to the skylights in the sharply sloping, iron roof.

He was in an artist's studio.

Zanna's studio.

Works stood propped against the walls. A half-finished canvas perched on an easel and there was a strong smell of oil paints and solvents. The overwhelming first impression that struck Nic was the sheer vitality of the colours around him. Muted, sun-baked hues in what looked like a series of work based on old European town streets that made him think of Italy and France. More vivid colours were in the flowers, like the deep blue of hydrangeas and the scarlet shades of poppies. Black cats could be seen concealed amongst the blooms. A series of sketches that the M&Ms must have inspired lay scattered on a table. Black cats—sleeping, washing themselves, jumping and playing. Even her pencil lines caught a sense of movement and vitality.

For a long, long time Nic didn't speak.

He didn't need to ask if she'd been the one who had painted that stunning row of sunflowers that made a dark hallway downstairs glow but it would have been an easy way to break the silence.

He actually opened his mouth to ask the rhetorical question but, as he did so, he shifted his gaze to where Zanna was standing and there was something about her stance that made the words evaporate.

Was she even aware of him being here?

CHAPTER FOUR

GOD…THIS WAS so much harder than she'd expected it to be.

She'd wanted him to fall in love with her beloved home. To understand why it was so important to save it. And this room was an integral piece of the architecture of the old house…

But it was so much more than that. The house was the home of her heart—where she felt loved, *safe*—but this room…

This was the room of her soul.

Her absolute refuge. It wasn't just paint smeared over those canvas sheets. They all contained fragments of *who* she was.

Not that he could know how much of a risk she was taking right now.

Zanna stared through the window as the shadows deepened but she couldn't see the huge rata trees below as they became dark and vaguely menacing shapes. There were other pictures in her mind.

Her best friend, Brianna, who'd travelled to London with her three years ago, when she'd graduated from art school. The bottle of champagne they'd splurged on when Brie had scored that job in a big gallery.

The show opening where she'd met Simon and fallen in love for the first time in her life. It had been a given that they would be living together within weeks. Planning their wedding and the rest of their lives.

More champagne as Brie and Simon had conspired to get Zanna to have her own show and they'd toasted her sparkling future as an artist. Not that she could show the *craft* that she'd previously engaged in, of course. Anyone could paint cute cats and flowers but they would coach her into producing *real* art. The kind that the critics would take notice of.

Had they known what kind of notice that would be taken? The humiliation of having her work ridiculed so publicly?

Of course they had. They'd been laughing about it that day, hadn't they? When she'd come home to find them in bed together.

Such a long, lonely trip back to New Zealand but it had been the only thing to do. She'd needed to heal and there had only been one place for that—in the comfort zone of her past. Maggie and the house. The shop with its magic and *this* room—the studio Maggie had created for her because she'd believed in her.

Even with all that faith and love and the solid grounding of the link to her past, it had taken a long time for her to climb those stairs again. To pick up a brush and start the work she had to do because it was who she was.

And now she'd allowed a stranger in here.

A potential critic.

Maybe she'd read too much into his impressions when he'd seen the sunflowers in the hallway and her immature efforts in the bathroom and on her bedroom walls. He might be too polite to reveal his opinion now that he was faced with her real work but she'd know the instant she looked at his face.

And she couldn't put it off any longer. Good grief… it felt like she'd been standing here for ever and there hadn't been a sound behind her.

She could hear something now, though. A quiet footfall on the bare, wooden floorboards. A long, slow inward breath. The faint squeak of leather in motion. By the time she turned, he was so close that she would see exactly what he was thinking. Especially with the way a last ray of the setting sun was angling directly through the window.

The unexpected explosion of colour as that sunbeam caught Zanna's hair took Nic's breath away and something else ignited deep in his belly, making arousal an overwhelming force.

Those astonishing eyes were wide. Vulnerable. She was waiting for his reaction to her art, wasn't she, but how could he begin to put the emotions they evoked into words?

To do so would mean opening a part of himself that he never looked at, let alone shared with anyone. The place where abandoned dreams were locked away. Where there was unconditional love and the warm comfort of a place called home.

Where a sunset meant far more than the passing of another day because you could shut off the rest of the world and simply be with the people who mattered most.

Nic felt like he was being dragged into that place—that's how much of an effect this room and what it contained had had on him.

Had he really intended to persuade Zanna to sell this property to him so that he could tear the house down to make way for something new?

Yes. It had to go, didn't it? It was a part of a dark past for him. A symbol of a time when the world had spun on its axis for a small boy and started the downward spiral to unbearable misery.

But it was part of Zanna's past, too. Part of who she was and she was…amazing.

There was too much to think about and it was too much of an emotional roller-coaster.

Confusing.

Right now, all Nic could think was that he wanted to make it all go away so that he could simply be with Zanna. If he could spend more time with her, maybe it would all fall into place.

He had to try and find some words. He couldn't just stand here and stare into her eyes.

'I…I don't know what to say,' he admitted. 'It's… You're…'

Something in her eyes seemed to melt. Were tears gathering? No…her lips softened as well, though you couldn't call it a smile. She lifted her hand. Placed a fingertip softly against his lips.

'You don't need to say anything,' she said softly. She drew in a breath, her next words no more than a sigh as she released it. 'Thank you…'

His hand captured hers and held it as she took it away. He lifted his other hand, without thinking, to mirror her action and touch *her* lips. Of their own accord, his fingers drifted sideways until they reached the angle of her jaw, with her chin cradled by his thumb.

Repercussions simply didn't exist in this moment. He

had to kiss her. That would undoubtedly make the rest of the world disappear, at least temporarily.

His touch was light. He would have felt the slightest flinch or withdrawal and there could be no mistaking his intentions as he slowly lowered his head so maybe she was feeling the same overwhelming pull?

The conviction that—unbeknownst to him, anyway—choices had already been made?

He was going to kiss her.

Or maybe he was merely responding to *her* desire to kiss him?

Why did she want it so badly?

Because it was a fitting way to thank him for the unspoken gift of validating her work? Words couldn't have encompassed what she'd seen in his eyes—the way her paintings had made him feel.

Because she needed so badly to have him on her side? To present a case that would not only mean that the house would be safe from the council's determination to get rid of it but that financial help would be available to restore Rata House to its former glory.

Maybe it was simply because she wanted to feel desirable again. That somebody wanted what she had to offer. That that somebody was the most gorgeous man she'd ever seen would only make it more special. Was that wrong enough to be ringing alarm bells?

Good grief, she could actually *hear* those bells as Nic's mouth hovered over hers, so close that she could feel their heat.

But then they got louder and Zanna gasped. She felt her mouth graze Nic's lips as she jerked her head sideways.

'It's the phone… I have to get that…' She was already

moving. She could see the stairs. 'It could be Maggie and the phone lines in Romania are awful.' She raised her voice as she flew down the narrow staircase. 'I've been worried about her for weeks.'

The spell had been broken and maybe that was for the best.

The memory of how he'd felt when he'd been a heartbeat away from kissing Zanna could be shoved into that space where the other broken things were stored. It would help if he got out of this room.

Nic shut the door of the studio behind him. When he reached the bottom of the spiral staircase he could hear her voice drifting up from somewhere downstairs.

'Maggie? Is that you? Oh, thank *goodness*... How are you? *Where* are you?'

Yes. The phone call had been timely. He could use a few minutes here to try and clear his head. Her voice got fainter, making it easy to tune it out as he paced the length of the hallway and back again and then paused beside a wide window at the end to peer out.

Maybe he needed to find a reconnection to the real world?

He could see his new acquisition from here—the ugly apartment block. It would be no great loss to the world to put a wrecking ball through that architectural disaster.

On the other side of Zanna's house was the small park where his first home and other cottages had long since been removed. If he *could* get this land, there couldn't be a more ideal place for the music school—bordered by the river and blending seamlessly into the pretty park. Perfect.

The motivation for the project was as strong as ever.

Unshakeable, in fact. This was something he *had* to do but there was no denying that niggle of guilt. That doubts were brewing.

This house might be a symbol of crushed dreams for him but for a lot of other people it was a symbol of something far more positive.

A place that inspired creativity.

A place to have their problems solved.

A place that oozed warmth.

Love…

Maybe that was where the doubts were originating. For the first time, Nic was tapping into memories that were worth cherishing. Feeling things he had denied himself for longer than he could remember. Would that portal be damaged if he obliterated the past to make a clean slate?

Compromise. Maybe that was the key.

What if he made a gallery of beautiful photographs in the entrance foyer to the school to honour the house that had been on this site? With a plaque to record its history and importance to a community that had long gone?

People could still visit.

Zanna could make a new studio somewhere else. He could help her find one.

He was still standing there, lost in thought, when Zanna came back up the stairs. 'We got cut off,' she said. 'But it doesn't matter. At least I know she's all right. More than all right, it seems.'

'Oh?' The sound was polite. His mind might be clearer now but his body was drifting back into a haze of desire. He had to consciously keep his hands on the windowsill behind him so that they didn't move in the hope of touching Zanna.

This was more than the kind of physical attraction he was used to. Maybe she really *was* a witch and he was the victim of some kind of bizarre manipulation.

Even her voice seemed to cast a spell.

'I didn't realise how worried I'd been, not hearing from her for so long. It's no wonder the phone lines are a bit of an issue, though. She's been in Bucharest and as far as the border to Ukraine near the Black Sea.'

Her hands seemed to be trying to follow an invisible map of Romania. She was speaking quickly and tiny flickers of her facial muscles added to the impression of vitality. *Passion…*

Did she look like this when she was immersed in her painting?

'Anyway, one of her second cousins runs some kind of a B&B. There was another guest there. A man called Dimitry. He owns a castle, it has no plumbing but I think she's in love…'

How had they managed to exchange so much information in such a short time? Was her aunt just as passionate in the way she talked or did they have the kind of connection that allowed communication on a level that needed very few words?

'With the castle or Dimitry?'

'She says it's the castle but I suspect it's both.'

Not that it mattered. Or maybe it did. In either case, surely a new dream would need funding. It could be an ace up his sleeve if the offer to buy this property was generous enough to allow for a new studio for Zanna and some money for her aunt to put into a castle restoration project as well.

'So she might not want to come back?'

The glow faded with disconcerting speed from Zanna's face. He could almost see her withdrawing—as if she'd revealed too much or said the wrong thing. She was putting up some kind of defensive barrier. Dammit. He wanted to see her smile again. To hear the voice that made him think of a rippling stream. To watch those compelling movements of her hands and face. But he couldn't even see her face now. She had taken a step forward to stare at the shadows of the world outside beyond his shoulder.

'It's probably just a holiday romance. There hasn't been anyone in her life for as long as I've known her. She's just…lonely…for something *I* can't give her.'

Nic's breath caught as he heard the echo of her tone. He had to turn towards her.

Was Zanna lonely, too?

There was a harsher note in her voice as she spoke again.

'Ugly, isn't it?'

He blinked. 'What is?'

'That apartment block next door. It's had nothing done to it for decades. The only people that live in it are the occasional squatters.'

'Needs pulling down.'

'That would cost money.' There was still passion in her voice but this was the flip side of the joy he'd heard when she'd been talking about her aunt. There was an undercurrent of something dark now. Something he could recognise all too easily.

Hatred. Contained but deeply rooted in the fear that something precious was going to be taken away from her.

'The owner doesn't want to spend that money until he gets what he *really* wants.'

'Which is?' The question was no more than a quiet prompt.

'*This* place. Enough land to make it worthwhile.'

Nic chose his words with care. 'You know the owner?'

'It's a company. Prime Property Limited. They specialise in development, though why they picked this place is a mystery. They usually make millions by ruining some gorgeous beach by building posh resorts. It's run by a man called Donald Scallion and his son, Blake. The scorpions, Maggie and I call them.' She flicked him a glance that might have been apologising for her tone. 'There's been…trouble…going back a fair few years now.'

'I'm sorry to hear that.'

It wasn't hard to make that sincere. This would all be so much easier if so much damage had not been done. It had been a mystery to Nic as well why Prime Property had bought the apartment block in the first place but if they hadn't, he wouldn't have seen that file sitting on Donald's desk when he'd come over to discuss another one of those lucrative resort developments they had worked together on more than once. He wouldn't have seen the image of a house he'd only seen in dreams for decades.

No. They'd been nightmares. Glimpses of the absolute security and happiness of his earliest years. People he couldn't touch and the sounds of music and laughter that he couldn't hear because of the invisible barrier that was closing in and suffocating him.

Now that mystery had taken a twist. It was only days ago that Donald had had his own turn to be mystified.

'Why on earth would you want it, Nic? It's a millstone.

The land's not big enough for a decent hotel and next door won't sell. We've tried everything, believe me...'

Nobody had to know why. Not yet.

Even Zanna?

Maybe especially Zanna.

The sincerity of his words was still hanging in the air between them. They had diffused the strength of Zanna's anger. That hatred. Flipped it, even?

Yes...the way she was looking at him now suggested that she believed he could help her.

And maybe he could. The image of one of the cards that had shocked him flashed into his head. That hanged man. She'd explained that a sacrifice could be needed sometimes. Something that would be difficult to give up but needed to go because it was blocking progress.

Maybe she just needed to understand...

But how could he persuade her? It was getting difficult to think again as her gaze held his so unwaveringly.

The spell...or force of attraction or whatever it was was gaining power again.

He wanted to persuade her...

He wanted her to understand...

He wanted...*her*.

It was as simple—and as complicated—as that. Maybe everything else could just wait a while longer.

He spoke quietly. 'Try not to worry, Zanna. Things will work themselves out.'

He could see hope in her eyes now. More than that. Faith? In *him*?

That gave him an odd squeeze of something he couldn't identify. Made him want to stand taller. Be a better person?

He could make this right in the end somehow. He could give Zanna what she needed.

Somewhere else.

Somewhere better.

It felt like he was floating, rather than consciously moving closer to Zanna. Close enough to touch. To pick up where they'd left off before the interruption of that phone call but, this time, he moved with a deliberate, delicious intent.

The curl in her hair had been enough to hold the braid together without any kind of fastening, the long end twisted into a perfect ringlet. He slipped his fingers into the braid just above the ringlet and, surprisingly, he could drag them down without meeting any resistance. Her hair was so soft it was easy to tease the coils apart as he worked his way up the long braid. His head was bent close to hers so he could whisper in her ear.

'Maybe you're not the only one who can see into the future.'

He'd reached the base of the silky rope that was virtually separating itself now, so that when he pushed his fingers through the thick waves, they touched the soft skin behind her ears. Impossible not to caress it. Zanna's inward breath was a tiny gasp.

'And perhaps it's a good thing that your aunt is having a break,' he continued. 'That she's found happiness.'

'With a man she's only just met?' Zanna's eyes had drifted shut. There was a tiny frown on her forehead as if she was trying to concentrate and he could see the effort she made to swallow. 'She's old enough to know better.'

Nic's hand was cradling that slim neck, locked in place by a soft tangle of copper waves. He lifted his other hand to trace the outlines of her face—drawing a fingertip with exquisite tenderness over each eyebrow, across her cheekbones, down the line of her jaw and, finally, over her lips.

'And you, Zanna?' he murmured. 'Are *you* old enough to know better?'

The touch of that fingertip was like the path of a slow-burning fuse.

Oh, yes…she was more than old and wise enough to know better. But there was a trail of fire that was sending heat throughout her entire body. She'd kept her eyes closed. Stifled a sigh that could have been one of pure pleasure escaping but the touch on her lips was too much. Her eyelids flickered open and it was a shock to find Nic's face so close to her own. To meet the gaze that was locked onto hers.

This man was a stranger. One who she might never see again after tonight. Only hours ago the idea of a one-night stand would have shocked her but that had been before the reawakening of physical desire that was so strong it was painful.

Deliciously painful.

She'd never felt it this strongly.

Maybe that was because she'd been so closed off since she'd left London. But maybe it was because this man had connected with her on a level that no one else ever had.

He understood her work.

He *got* her.

It felt like they'd already connected on an intimate level. What would it be like to make that connection physical as well as emotional?

His eyes were darkened to black by a desire she recognised instantly because she was sharing it. Her lips parted to utter the word that should have been the only sane response to his soft query but no word emerged. Instead, her tongue touched that fingertip and her lips closed again, taking it prisoner.

Had he groaned, or had that sound of unbearable need come from somewhere inside herself? The tension was morphing into movement and Zanna braced herself for an explosive release of whatever was containing that shared desire. This kiss had the potential to be uncontrollable and bruising.

But when his lips touched hers, that first time, they did so with a softness that was heartbreakingly tender. A totally unexpected gentleness. A tiny gap of time and the pressure increased to soar into something as uncontrollable as she'd anticipated. A taste of something new and powerful enough to be frightening in its intensity but that tiny gap of time couldn't be erased.

It had only been a heartbeat of such gentleness but it had been long enough to win her trust.

She was lost.

Her bedroom.

It was the obvious choice, given that its door was open just down the hallway and it offered a surface where they could resume this amazing kiss without the distraction of having to stay standing.

Taking her hand by threading his fingers through hers, Nic led Zanna into the room with the painted garden of a thousand flowers. *Her* room. He felt the sudden tension in her hand that could have become hesitation and he lifted it smoothly to her neck, keeping their fingers locked as he kissed her again, his tongue dancing with hers. Then he released her hand, using his own to hook the hem of her top to lift it and peel it off over her head.

The scrap of orange fabric fell to the floor and Zanna felt his hands tracing the knobs at the top of her spine. Shaping the dip of her shoulder blades and ribs and then sliding around and coming up so that his thumbs slid over the curve of her breasts and grazed nipples already so hard they ached. The brief stroke sent an exquisitely painful jolt of sensation that went straight to another ache building much lower, in her core.

Did he sense that? She could feel the strength and purpose in those large hands as they went to the fastening of her jeans. He popped the stud but didn't touch the zipper, merely holding the waistband and pulling to separate the fabric. Zanna heard the groan of the metal teeth parting and then his hands were on her back again, sliding beneath the denim. Beneath the flimsy fabric of her knickers so that he was cupping bare skin.

Dear Lord…she had never done anything like this in her entire life. Sex with a total stranger.

Except he didn't feel like a stranger. Some sort of connection had been there from that first moment, hadn't it? The way he'd looked at her after he'd spent all that time looking at her paintings. A haunted—and haunt*ing*—look. He'd been touched in a deep place.

A tender place. As tender as that first kiss that had won her trust had been.

Even after months together, Simon had never been able to touch her like this. To touch her body or her soul like this. But Nic *was* still a stranger. A gorgeous stranger who was, clearly, a very accomplished lover. This was new—and dangerous—but instead of making her want to run and hide, it was simply adding another dimension that made it irresistible.

Until now, she'd merely clung to him, the passage of time irrelevant. There was no going back. Zanna wanted it all.

And she wanted it *now.*

'Nic...'

The hoarse whisper was a plea that he couldn't refuse. Going as slowly as he might have liked was no longer an option as he felt her hands slide from his neck to fumble with the buckle of his belt.

He could give her exactly what she wanted. What they both wanted.

He caught her hands and held them. Tipped her back towards the bed and let her fall gently, catching her jeans as she slid through his hands to tug them free.

He stripped off his leather jacket, reaching into the pocket in the lining to extract the small, foil packet he knew was there. He saw the way her eyes widened. Did she think he carried a condom because he made a habit of spur-of-the-moment sex with a complete stranger?

The assumption would be wrong. He might have had the opportunity—more than once—but he'd never indulged in meaningless encounters.

Including now. How this had become so meaningful in such a short blink of time was beyond his comprehension but he wasn't going to waste a moment more than it took to shed his clothes by trying to think about it.

He didn't want to think about anything other than this amazing woman. How she would feel and taste as he made love to her. What he would see in those incredible eyes as he took them both into paradise.

CHAPTER FIVE

SPELLBOUND...

Maybe there *was* some kind of magic in the air around here.

That could explain the vivid dream Nic had just woken from and the way his hand reached out to see if the woman he'd just been kissing so intensely in his sleep was actually real. To try and keep feelings he hadn't known existed pumping through his body for a bit longer?

But the other side of the bed was empty. Still warm but empty. As though someone had waved a wand and made Zanna simply vanish into thin air. The fragments of that dream became elusive and evaporated into the air as well. An overall impression of the last hours remained, however, and it had been—easily—the most memorable night of his life so far.

That pleasure also seemed destined to evaporate as Nic opened his eyes and blinked in the morning light. He was alone in a strange bed and he had potentially made a complicated mess of what should have been a straightforward business proposition.

He needed to buy this house and then put a bulldozer through it.

Admittedly, that would come after salvaging some

of the architectural antiques but there was no getting around the fact that he would be destroying this house.

Zanna's house.

Guilt took a hefty swipe at him out of left field. Something about this house had been absorbed enough to get under his skin. Or maybe it was something about Zanna that he'd absorbed.

Tasted and revelled in, more likely.

Mon Dieu...

Nic threw the bed covers back and pushed himself to his feet. He'd find that ivy-covered bathroom and take a quick shower. It would be helpful if he was fully clothed and couldn't smell Zanna Zelenksy on his skin before he initiated the conversation he needed to have with her.

The one where he persuaded her to sell him her house.

There was still no sign of Zanna as Nic went downstairs a short time later and he could feel the emptiness of the big old house. Not that it felt oppressive. However unhelpful it was to think about it, houses like this had real character and this one gave him a picture of an elderly and much-loved grandmother in a rocking chair, quite content with what life had to offer and waiting patiently, knowing that there were more good things to come.

Oblivious to the fact that there was a time for everything to die?

It didn't have to die, though, did it? Nic had the power to save a life here. The ridiculous notion was dismissed with a grunt. This was a *house*. If he wanted to wallow in the analogy of life and death, all he needed to do was focus on the birth of the new and beautiful creation that would take the place of this outdated dwelling.

Yes, Zanna would hate him for it but that wasn't his

problem, was it? It wasn't as if he'd ever see her again after his business was concluded here. His life was in Europe and New Zealand was a whole world away. There were countless other beautiful women in that world. He didn't have to forget about her—she could just join the ranks of others who had briefly touched his life in a memorable fashion.

Except she was nothing like any of the others, was she?

Her beauty was unique with that flame-coloured hair and those extraordinary eyes and milky skin. Her passion was unique, too. Her talent mind-blowing.

She's flaky, he reminded himself. Her unusual bloodline and upbringing put her on the outskirts of what rational people would find acceptable. An outcast, almost.

That wasn't helping to clear his head.

Nic knew what it felt like to be an outcast.

The kitchen was deserted but the French doors to the garden were open so Nic went outside. Into the bricked courtyard garden beyond the French doors. There was a wrought-iron table and chairs here and a clay chiminea that looked as though it was well used as an outside fire. A clear blue sky held the promise of a beautiful day but it was early enough for it to still be a little crisp. Following a brick pathway through an arch that was almost invisible beneath a riot of dark red roses, he turned a corner to find Zanna crouched in a large vegetable garden.

She was wearing those jeans again that clung to her long legs like a second skin but the orange top had gone today. Today's choice was a close-fitting, white singlet and, from this angle, Nic was getting a view of cleavage that took his mind straight back to the pleasures of last night. He wouldn't have thought it was possible but it had been even better the second time…

Layered over the singlet was an unbuttoned, canary-yellow shirt. Another flame colour to tone with her hair and that sharpened the memories of the heat that had been generated between them. The sleeves of the shirt were rolled up to her elbows and her hair was loose—the way he liked it best.

Whoa…the thought had an edge of possessiveness. Permanence, even. How disturbing was that?

And suddenly this had all the awkwardness of the morning after, with the need to escape without causing offence, compounded by the guilt of knowing he had infiltrated a rival's camp under false pretences.

He cleared his throat. 'Hey, there…'

'Hi, Nic.' Zanna stood up with graceful ease, a fistful of greenery in her hand. 'I was finding some parsley. I thought you might like some scrambled eggs for breakfast?'

One of the black cats appeared from beneath the giant leaf of a rambling pumpkin vine to rub against his ankle. Then it flopped onto its back, inviting a tummy scratch.

'I've never seen him do that before.' Zanna stepped carefully between the splashes of colour a row of marigolds made. The other two cats were close on her heels. 'Merlin really likes you.'

'You sound surprised.'

'He's very picky when it comes to people.' Smiling, she kept moving until she stood close enough for her body to touch his. Then she stood on tiptoe and lifted her face. Nic felt the bunch of parsley tickle his ear as she kissed him lightly. 'Just like me.'

The touch of her lips was a spell all on its own. For

a few seconds it was enough to wipe out the awkwardness. Enough to shove that guilt into a mental cupboard and slam the door. Nic slid his hands beneath the yellow shirt and held Zanna's waist as he kissed her back. Disturbing echoes of warnings that he was only making things worse faded to nothing as he was sucked back into the present moment. The softness of those lips and the feel of her breasts against his chest...

Zanna felt the parsley slip from her fingers as the kiss took her straight back to last night.

The most amazing night of her life.

The strength of this attraction and her response to it was unnerving. Unreal. She could feel herself being dragged back into a place where nothing else mattered and no one else existed. Fighting the distraction was difficult but it had to be done. She knew she was risking too much, too soon, to trust how he made her feel. Not only that, she'd made a resolution out here in the garden—to talk to Nic about why he was really here. To be honest about how much they needed the financial help a historical protection order could provide.

To ask for his help...

'Eggs,' she murmured against Nic's lips. 'Scrambled,' she added a few seconds later.

'Mmm. With parsley.'

'It's here somewhere.' Zanna slipped free of his arms, crouching to collect the fallen sprigs.

They walked past the old apple and pear trees on the small lawn that divided the vegetable garden from the courtyard beyond the archway. The cats stayed as close as they could to her feet without getting stepped on.

'Look at that. The grass is almost dead. Which reminds me, I need to give the rata trees a good drink.

This is the best time of day to put some water on. Do you mind waiting a bit longer for breakfast?'

'You don't have to cook for me.'

'I'd like to.' Zanna looked up. 'There's something I'd like to talk to you about.'

He held her gaze. 'I've got something I'd like to talk to you about, too.'

Her heart skipped a beat. Could it be that they were on the same page? That she wouldn't even have to ask for his help because he already intended to offer it?

Leaving the parsley on the arm of a wooden bench seat, Zanna headed for the front of the house and Nic followed her. He needed a few minutes to think about what he was going to say and it was helpful to catalogue more of the degeneration of the building as they walked. The paint wasn't just peeling, it was clearly falling off rotten weatherboard. Guttering was hanging loose and he could see the remnants of broken roof tiles pushing more of it out of place. It wouldn't be that long before the house was uninhabitable.

The hose lay coiled like a solid snake near the outside tap. The sprinkler was inside a galvanised bucket with hose attachments and an old iron key. He held it up.

'Lost something?'

'No. It's the spare for the front door. Maggie's a great one for losing keys and she's convinced nobody would think of looking in the bucket. Leave it there. The sprinkler's all we need at the moment.'

She showed him where to place it. They stood under the rata trees amidst a steady drift of leaves and one of the cats took a swipe as a leaf fell nearby.

'Good grief…it's *raining* leaves.' Nic was staring up at the canopy of the tree. He shaded his eyes with his hand, already well into a damage-locating frame of mind but this was an unexpected bonus. 'What's *that*?'

'What?'

Nic moved to touch the trunk. Nearly hidden by the twisted bark was a large hole.

'If that hole was made by a beetle, I hope I don't come across it. It's *huge*.'

'There's another one.' Nic pointed further up the trunk. He stepped out of sight behind the tree. 'And there's more.'

'No wonder the trees are looking sick. They're infested.'

Nic's face appeared again. 'I don't think it's beetles.' Going back to the first hole at head level, he ran his fingers around its edge.

'These holes have been deliberately drilled,' he said quietly. 'And I'm guessing they've been filled with some kind of poison.'

Zanna could feel the blood drain from her face. 'Who would do something that awful?' she whispered. 'These trees are so special. A lot of people supported the bid to have them protected. There was quite a fuss about it and it was an election year so the city council had to take some notice.'

'How long ago did that happen?'

'Ages. Before I went to London. Maybe five or six years ago? Just after the apartment block was sold and we started having trouble, I guess.'

'If someone had been upset about the decision to have the trees protected and did something, it's more than long enough for poison to have an effect, even on such big trees. Let's have a look at the other one and see what we're up against.'

We?

Was this a declaration of whose side Nic was on?

The shock was wearing off by the time they returned to the kitchen but Zanna didn't bother collecting the parsley on the way past. She felt sick. Grief and anger twisted themselves into a painful knot in her belly.

'There's no hope for them, is there? Either of them.'

'I wouldn't think so.' Nic was watching her intently. 'Someone's done a thorough job.'

'What's it going to be next? Will they poison the cats to try and drive us away?'

He gave her an odd look. 'Nobody's going to poison your cats, Zanna.'

'You don't know that. They warned me that they'd win in the end.'

'Who?'

'The scorpions. Prime Property. The owners of the horrible apartment block next door. They want this land and, clearly, they're going to use any means they can to get it.'

He turned away from her and paced a couple of steps as though he didn't want to have any more to do with this situation.

Well…why would he? He'd been sent here to do a simple job and it was suddenly getting complicated and unpleasant.

What if last night had only been a one-night stand as far as Nic was concerned? If the prospect of emotional involvement sent him running for the hills? Maybe he was appalled at the thought of dealing with a weeping woman.

Zanna might be more than a little upset but she wasn't about to burst into tears.

She was angry. And it was too easy to turn at least a

part of that anger onto someone who wanted to simply walk away. What had happened to that *we* he'd mentioned?

When Nic turned back to face her, he knew his face was grim. This was the time to tell her a few home truths. That the trees would have to be felled. That the house was disintegrating around her. That the only sensible thing to do was to take an offer that would be generous enough to make it easy to move on to something that wouldn't generate increasingly stressful problems.

'No, they're not.' Tension made the words come out as almost a snap. 'They're not even in the picture any more. But—'

'How would *you* know?' Zanna's voice rose as she interrupted him. The flash in her eyes made him remember just how passionate this woman could be. And she was being threatened now, albeit in an underhanded way that had probably happened a long time ago. It might have had nothing to do with the Scallions' determination to acquire the property. Maybe there was someone out there who simply didn't like trees.

'Because…' Nic ran his fingers through his hair, blowing out a breath as he looked away from her again. 'Zanna…I…' He was struggling to think of what to say. *Because I own that apartment block now?* He could see exactly where that would go. She would see him as no more than the replacement of a Prime Property representative. Somebody determined to force her to give up her property. And she'd be right.

It would hurt her and…dammit, maybe it had to happen but he didn't have to like hurting her, did he?

And…maybe—just maybe—there was a way around this. A solution…

He could feel the way she was staring at him but the idea was embryonic and there was no point even suggesting it if it wasn't possible. He wasn't even thinking about her now. His mind was racing. He had a lot of work to do before he would know if this idea had merit.

Zanna could feel her eyes narrowing. He was looking for an excuse to get away, wasn't he? Fine. She had other people to worry about.

'How am I going to break this news to Maggie?' She didn't expect an answer. 'She'll be heartbroken. She'll feel like she has to come home and that'll spoil a trip of a lifetime for her.'

'Zanna… Listen to me. I—'

But she didn't want to hear any more of his well-intentioned reassurances. Not when he didn't actually care. Or have a clue how serious this was. She held up a hand as a signal to stop him speaking. She needed time to think. To get past this visceral reaction and plan what to do about it. A glance at the wall clock made the means of finding that time easy.

'It's nearly nine o'clock. You'll have to excuse me. I have to open the shop.'

She wasn't going to let him say anything, was she? His best intentions of letting her know that he wasn't the person she thought he was and that he had his own interests in this property were fading with every interruption.

'I've got things I need to do as well.' Nic followed her gaze at the clock, then he looked at the door.

Zanna shook her head. He really couldn't wait to get away, could he?

'Did you need anything else from me?'

A split second of searing eye contact reminded her of what he'd needed from her last night. What she'd needed from *him*. But it was gone so quickly she could have been mistaken.

'What?'

'The house. Did you need anything else?' He would need to file a report on the historical value of the house, wouldn't he? 'Like any documents or photos?'

Oddly, he blinked as if he had no idea what she was talking about. Then he closed his eyes slowly and nodded.

Of course. He was well down a new track mentally but Zanna still thought he was here on behalf of a historical protection society to document the merits of preserving this old house. And, thanks to the shock of finding the trees had been poisoned, she was so focused on the immediate issue that she would automatically block any suggestion of stepping back to look at the bigger picture.

Nic could see it very clearly and it gave him a completely different angle on which he might be able to base his pitch. He already had a dozen things buzzing in his own head that needed attention. They could talk later. When she'd had some time to calm down and he was armed with more information.

'Yeah... A few photos might be useful. I'll use the camera on my phone.'

Disappointment was just as strong as her anger. Painful, even. He would walk out the door any minute now and that might be the last time she ever saw him. She couldn't help the chilliness of her next words.

'That's not very professional, is it?'

'Sorry?'

'I would have thought that an official report would need more than that.' She gave an incredulous huff. 'How many jobs like this have you actually done, Nic?'

Good grief…how frustrating was this? He couldn't afford to tell her the truth now. She'd throw him out on his ear and he'd never get a second chance. 'I do know what I'm doing, Zanna.'

She'd annoyed him now. Oh, help… How had things changed so dramatically in such a short time? It seemed like only minutes ago that the world had stopped turning while they'd been kissing in the vegetable garden and now here they were, practically glaring at each other. This clearly wouldn't be a good time to ask for his help, then.

A flash of pure desperation made her open her mouth to do just that or at least to ask if she was going to see him again but Nic wasn't even looking at her. Was he trying to work out how to access the camera on his phone?

Words failed her.

What would she say? *It was nice to meet you* or *Thanks for last night and how 'bout you write a report that will help me save my house?*

Would he think that she'd offered him her body as some kind of bribe?

She could feel her colour rising. It was her turn to look away now. To eye the door as a means of escape.

'Well…you'll know where to find me if you need anything else, I guess. Just pull the front door closed when you're done. It'll lock itself.'

CHAPTER SIX

ZANNA HEARD THE ROAR of a powerful motorbike being revved a short time later as she finished lighting the candles on the counter.

So he was gone.

He'd made her feel so special.

Desirable.

Talented.

Loved...

A few hours. No more than a blip in a lifetime but she knew she would never forget those hours for as long as she lived.

They had been precious and they should be enough.

He'd given her two amazing gifts. He'd reawakened desire. So effectively that Zanna knew it was going to be possible to fall in love again. He'd shown her that there was an oasis in the desert it felt like her heart had become.

And he'd given her faith in her art again. Her real art.

Either one of those gifts were priceless. She should be feeling enormously grateful instead of this crushing sense of loss that she would never see Nic again. An almost desperate longing for more...

People came and went in the shop. Being so close to

the central city, there were a lot of hotels nearby and tourists were drawn to the anachronism of the old, dilapidated house that didn't belong where it was any more. They didn't buy much but at least the distraction was enough to stop her thinking so much about Nic.

The day still dragged, however, and Zanna had to try hard to keep focused. She smiled at the tourists and wondered if stocking a few souvenir items like kiwi toys and paua shells might help the profit margin. No. Maggie would hate that. She still mourned the time when Spellbound had been more about the tearoom and the people who'd come together here.

But they both had to make a living. More than make a living. Somehow, they'd have to find enough money to deal with the trees. To do something more than temporarily patch up the worst of the damage time was doing to the house. Manuka honey that was known for its medicinal properties wouldn't be so out of place amongst their stock. Zanna needed to ring her essential oil supplier among others today. Maybe one of them would know a reliable source for the honey.

By late afternoon, she'd had enough. The arrival of the teenage girls who'd been here yesterday made her spirits sink even further. They weren't genuine customers, any more than Nic had been. And they'd been in the shop when he'd arrived so it was impossible not to think of him. To cast a glance at the door with the forlorn hope that history might repeat itself and he would be the next person to appear.

'Jen wanted another look at that book of spells,' the dark-haired girl explained. 'The little blue one.'

'Knock yourselves out.'

It was quiet for a few minutes. Zanna breathed in

the lavender of the oil she had chosen today in the hope of calming her mind. It didn't seem to be working. She still felt churned up about the discovery of the poisoned trees. Maybe she should burn a bit of sage to eliminate any lingering negative energy. Except that it was more likely that a good part of that uncomfortable sensation was stemming from knowing she wouldn't be seeing Nic again and sage wasn't going to help.

'Hey, this is cool.' The girl sounded excited. 'You can make Stevie call you, Jen. Look—it's easy. First you just have to choose a colour that represents him.'

'How do I do that?' The blonde girl called Jen directed her question at Zanna rather than her friend.

'There's a colour chart in the book.' Zanna automatically went to help them, taking the book and flicking through the pages. 'Here. You choose a colour that represents his characteristics.'

'Stevie's orange for sure,' Jen declared, moments later. 'Able to make friends readily. Generally good-natured, likeable and social.'

Orange was her favourite colour. Would she pick it to represent Nic's characteristics? Likeable was too insipid a word to apply to him. With his beauty combined with that confidence and ability to display tenderness, the attraction went way beyond *liking* him. It would be all too easy to fall head over heels in love with him.

Maybe she already had…

'I reckon he's red,' her friend countered. 'They form opinions rapidly, express them boldly and choose sides quickly but may be swayed easily from one viewpoint to another.'

Nic could be red. He was certainly bold. It had felt like he'd chosen her side, too. Had he changed his mind when it had become apparent that the road might get a bit too rocky?

'Stevie's not loud enough to be red.'

'He's your boyfriend, I guess. Or he will be—if this spell works.' The girl grinned at Zanna. '*Does* it really work?'

'I haven't tried it.'

Maybe she should…

'So what do I do now that I've picked the colour?' Jen sounded breathless.

'You've got a photo of Stevie, haven't you?'

'Yeah…I cut it out of the school magazine.'

'Okay, then. You need some orange thread and an orange jellybean and the photo. You tie the thread around the photo and leave it for at least one hour to absorb his energy. Then you use the same thread to tie the jellybean to your phone.'

'And then what?'

'And then he rings you up and asks for a date, of course.'

'Oh…' She looked at Zanna with a hopeful expression. 'Do you sell jellybeans?'

'No. There's a petrol station down the end of Rata Avenue. They'll have some.'

'Hey, thanks so much.' Jen's smile was shy. 'I'll let you know if it works.'

'Good luck.'

With the excited energy of the young girls gone, the shop became almost oppressive and time slid by even more slowly.

What did you do with massive, dying trees? Would they turn into skeletons that would make the house look like a Halloween prop or would some official person come and say that they were required to have them taken down because they could present a danger to the public?

How much would that cost?

She wouldn't tell Maggie about it, Zanna decided. She couldn't bring herself to dampen the joy her aunt was experiencing. She'd been left in charge. More than that, because Maggie had signed a power of attorney, giving her absolute control over everything to do with the house and shop while she was overseas. And the trees had probably been on death row for years. A few more months wouldn't make any difference.

It was simply another obstacle to overcome. It wasn't the final straw—not by a long shot.

Zanna picked up the book of spells the girls had left on the counter and went to put it back on the display shelf. She could close up soon and go back into the house. She needed to do some baking. The organic chocolate-chip cookies were always popular. So was the banana bread. Would it be better than being in the shop with the ghost of Nic's energy lurking?

No. It would probably be worse. There could be far more of that energy lingering in the hallway where he'd given her that first gift of knowing that her art was meaningful…

In the kitchen where she'd read his cards…

In her bedroom…

Zanna closed her eyes, trying to gather some inner strength.

And then she heard it. The roar of a powerful engine in the street.

The silence that followed was enough for her to be able to hear her own heartbeat as it picked up speed and thumped against her ribs.

He'd come back.

The joy of that knowledge took her breath away.

The bell on the door jangled.

'Hey…' Nic's tone was light but there was an underlying tension that was still making it impossible to breathe. 'You're due to close, aren't you?'

Zanna could only nod. She stared as he stepped closer. He had his helmet tucked under his arm but he had something else in his other hand. Another helmet.

'Put this on,' Nic directed. 'And come with me. There's something I want to show you.'

Zanna had never been on a motorbike. She had no idea where Nic might be planning to take her or what it was he wanted to show her.

This was crazy but she felt her hand reaching out to take the helmet.

It didn't feel like she had a choice. Or maybe that choice had already been made, in that instant when she'd invited Dominic Brabant to step into her life.

This time, Zanna could feel as well as hear the engine as Nic kick-started it into life with her sitting on the back of the bike. She'd been so sure that she'd never see him again when she'd heard it only that morning but the shocked delight of hearing him return had blown that misery out of the water.

Now she had the rich rumble of the huge machine between her legs and her arms tightly wound around Nic's waist with her chest pressed against his back. It felt dangerous and wildly exciting and incredibly sexy. She could see the road flashing past the wheels and feel the ends of her hair whipping in the wind. The first time he leaned into a corner and she felt the bike tipping was terrifying but then they were upright again and she was safe.

Because she was with Nic.

He'd come back and she felt safe again.

It took very little time to weave through the rush-hour traffic of the central city and then cut across one of the outer suburbs. This was the green belt where the wealthy could have lifestyle blocks and indulge hobbies like breeding alpacas or making boutique wines. A gorgeous, lush valley with hills and a river and pockets of native bush like small forests.

Halfway along the winding road the bike slowed and turned through some old, ornate wooden gates. They rolled past a small lake bordered by weeping willows that had a faded, wooden rowboat moored by a miniature jetty. An ancient, stone building that might have been stables long ago had a backdrop of tall, native trees but at the end of the pebbled driveway, there was nothing but a smooth stretch of grass like an inner-city park.

What on earth did he want to show her?

A perfect spot for a romantic picnic? It seemed unlikely that the small storage compartment on the bike could be hiding a hamper.

Climbing off the bike, Zanna was already missing the contact of Nic's body but his hands brushed her neck and jawline as he helped ease the helmet off her head. Even better, he then dipped his head and kissed her.

Long and slow. With that mind-blowing tenderness that had captured her heart so completely.

It was hard to suck in a breath. Even harder to think of something to say. She could feel her lips curving into a smile.

'Nice. But you could have shown me that anywhere.'

He took her hand. 'Come with me.'

They didn't stop until they'd walked up the gentle slope to reach the middle of the grassed area. Nic was still holding her hand but he wasn't looking at her. His gaze travelled slowly to take in the whole scene from top of the hill to the lake and the patch of forest and the old stables. His nod was satisfied.

'It's as good as they told me it was,' he said. 'Perfect.'

'It's certainly gorgeous,' she agreed. 'Idyllic. But what's it perfect for?'

'A house. This land is for sale. Not on the open market yet but when it is, it'll be marketed internationally. It's special, isn't it?'

Zanna blinked. Was Nic thinking of buying this property? 'You're going to build a house? You want to *live* here?'

His expression was unreadable. 'The idea of having a New Zealand summer instead of a European winter every year is certainly attractive but, no, I'm not thinking of building a house.' It looked like he was taking a deep breath. 'I was thinking of helping someone to *shift* a house.'

Zanna's jaw dropped. An image of Rata House on this land appeared in her head with astonishing clarity. With space all around instead of being dwarfed by high-rise buildings. Air to breathe that wasn't full of the fumes of inner-city traffic. A garden that could include a whole orchard instead of a couple of tired fruit trees. The serenity of a view that encompassed a tranquil lake and cool, shady forest. Stables that could be a gallery or beautiful tea rooms.

A dream scenario but…it simply wasn't possible.

The shake of her head felt violent enough to send a

painful twinge down her spine. She let go of Nic's hand as if it was burning her and stepped backwards to create more distance.

'No...'

'I know it's a big idea.' Nic was watching her carefully. 'You need a bit of time to get used to it.'

Zanna shook her head again. 'You're wrong. It's not a new idea. Someone suggested it years ago and Maggie was really upset about it. She said the damage would be too great and the spirit of joy from all the lives that had touched the house would be broken. It's what it is because it's *where* it is.'

'No.' His gaze was steady. Compelling. 'It's what it is because of the lives that have touched it and that's happened because of the people who live in it.' Nic's voice was quiet. As calm as his face. 'But it's dying slowly because of where it is. Getting more and more hemmed in and out of place and you must know how much it's crying out for some restoration. Wouldn't it be better to save it? Shifting it would be the ideal opportunity to repair and strengthen it. You and Maggie could still live in it. Still have the shop and the tea rooms. The people who know the house could still visit. It's not that far.'

'It's too big. It couldn't be done.'

'Anything's possible. I have a mate—Pete Wellesley—who's a specialist in shifting houses. He owes me a favour. I have tickets on hold and he could fly over from Sydney first thing tomorrow to have a look. He's already seen the photographs I took and he reckons it's doable. They'd take off the roof and turret and cut the house into pieces, separating the floors. Then they'd put new foundations down on the new site and put it all back together. With enough people on the job it would only take a few weeks.'

'It would cost a fortune.'

'The land it's on is worth a fortune. I could make sure you get enough to cover any costs.'

'Why?' Zanna's head was spinning. There was too much to think about. 'Why are you doing all this?'

He hesitated for a long moment. 'I want to help. And I know what's going to happen.'

It was what she'd wanted, wasn't it? To persuade him to help? This wasn't what she'd had in mind, though. And there was something ominous in his tone.

'What do you mean—what's going to happen?'

'I've been talking to people on the city council today.'

Of course he had. It was what he'd been employed for.

'And?'

'There's been an unofficial vote that could become official very shortly. The council feels that the house is in the way of what could be an important development for the inner city. Their words were that it was interfering with their approved developmental mission for the inner city. They could enforce a sale to them and the value they would assign is likely to be a lot less than what it would be worth if you sold it privately. Also, any legal costs of trying to object would be taken out of a compensation package.' He was holding her horrified gaze. 'The clock's ticking, Zanna. Time's running out.'

She was so scared.

Oh, she was holding herself admirably straight and the tilt of her chin suggested she would fight to the death for something—or someone—she loved but Nic could see the fear in her eyes.

The need to protect her was overwhelming. The beautiful thing was that he could do that without hurting his own interests. This was a win-win situation for everybody involved. He'd spent the day networking harder than he ever had on a project. Finding the right people to talk to and calling in favours from all over the show but he'd pulled it together. The germ of the idea he'd had that morning was coming together so smoothly that it felt like it was meant to happen.

Just as surely as Zanna Zelensky had been meant to come into his life?

Right on the heels of the need to protect came the urge to comfort and reassure. It took only a step or two to fold Zanna into his arms and hold her close. She needed time, that was all. The solution was here—for all of them. It was a stroke of extremely good fortune—and his inside contacts in the real estate industry—that had made this piece of the countryside available and Zanna had seen it without being prejudiced by knowing the agenda. She would see the location of her beloved house through a very different lens when he took her back there now because she wouldn't be able to help imagining it here.

He knew better than to push too hard. This was the time to back off. As counter-intuitive as it seemed on the surface, he needed to actually distract Zanna and let the concept take root subconsciously. He could take her out to dinner somewhere. Take her home and make love to her again. And again.

His arms tightened around her.

It might be part of an automatic game plan but it was also a bonus he wasn't about to resist, despite the niggle of the guilt that hadn't been entirely vanquished by working on this superb solution.

He hadn't said a word that wasn't the truth. He just hadn't told her the whole story—that the development the council members were so excited about was the concept of his music school. That planning permission would be a given and that enforcing a sale of Rata House would only be set into action if he had problems acquiring the necessary extra land.

He could wait and purchase the land from the council, probably for less than he intended to offer now. He was doing *this* part purely for Zanna. He'd also told the truth when he'd said the house was slowly dying. They couldn't afford the repairs it needed and they were unlikely to get council permission for any major structural work even if they could have afforded it. He did want to help. To look after her. He knew better than to put her back up by voicing the desire, however. This was a woman who could look after herself and instinct told him it was going to be tricky to win her complete trust.

While he couldn't allow it to jeopardise his project, the desire to win her trust was surprisingly strong.

And bubbling somewhere beneath the fire he'd thrown all those irons into today was the idea that it might be simple to merely fudge a timeframe. If he'd acquired the apartment block *after* buying the Zelenksy property then nobody—well, a particular somebody that he was holding close right now—could accuse him of having a conflict of interest.

Could it even be considered a conflict when it was such a perfect solution?

Yes, he was treading a fine line but it wasn't the first time. The biggest risks often generated the biggest rewards.

Time *was* running out. He'd allowed himself a week

to sort this project. It was only day two and if he could pull it off, he was on track so that everybody could win. Even better, he would have a whole week with Zanna that he could remember for the rest of his life.

'Let's go home,' he whispered into her ear. 'And sleep on it.'

Nic wouldn't let her talk about it that evening.

'Wait until you have all the information you need,' he said. 'Until the idea stops spinning in your head for long enough to see it properly. I've given Pete the nod to jump on a plane in the morning. He'll be able to answer questions better than me. Then it'll be time to talk.'

He distracted her, instead. With food and wine, at a gorgeous restaurant that had beautiful music and a dance floor.

It was no surprise that this astonishing man could dance so well. What was a surprise was the sheer bliss of drifting in his arms to the music. Of being with him.

Of wanting to be with him...for ever?

That made her head spin as much as the crazy idea of shifting her home to the most idyllic location possible.

They were dreams. Too good to be believable.

Either of them.

But, oh...it was heaven to play with them for a while.

He wasn't going to let her sleep on the concept in a hurry either, when they finally returned to Zanna's bed.

They were comfortable with each other's bodies now. Enough to touch and explore and discover new things. Nic's leisurely tracing of her body came to a halt as his fingers brushed the stone in her navel.

'I meant to ask last night,' he murmured. 'What is it?'

'A topaz,' she told him. 'My birth stone.'

'It's perfect for you. It's got the colours of flames in it. Just like your hair.' He stroked a soft curl back from her face. 'And your eyes…' He moved in to kiss her softly and she felt her lips curl beneath his.

'Why are you smiling?'

'This stone is supposed to enhance emotional balance.'

His lips were so close she could feel the word more than hear it. 'And?'

'And I'm not feeling particularly balanced right now.'

There was a moment of absolute stillness then. As if the world was holding its breath—waiting for her to tell him that she was in love with him?

She couldn't. Not yet. It was all too new to trust and too big to mess with. But it was hanging there, unspoken.

'Same,' Nic whispered.

Another moment of stillness could have made the atmosphere way too intense but then she felt his lips curl into a smile.

'I think I like it.'

Zanna was more than ready to sink into the kiss. 'Same.'

CHAPTER SEVEN

SLEEP HAD FINALLY come but the first fingers of light from a new dawn found Zanna awake again.

Her head was still spinning.

Or maybe it wasn't. Maybe her head was just fine and it was the world spinning around her. Changing its axis. Presenting her with possibilities that should be elusive and only dreams but were actually close enough to touch.

Nic was close enough to touch. Sprawled on his back with one arm flung above his head. For a long minute Zanna simply gazed at him. She loved the rumpled disorder of his wavy hair and the tangle of dark lashes kissing the top of those chiselled cheekbones. His lips were slightly parted and so deliciously soft looking amidst the dark shadowing of his jaw she had to consciously stop herself reaching out to touch them.

Instead, she slipped quietly from the bed. She needed a bit of time to herself to walk around the house and think. To compose a careful text message that wouldn't panic Maggie and make her think she had to come home but would still let her know that there was some urgency to make some big decisions.

It was Saturday, which meant she could close the shop

at midday and that would be about the time Nic returned from collecting Pete from the airport. They had the rest of the day before Pete's return flight to Sydney but the pressure was going to be on for her to make some kind of decision by the time he left, at least on whether or not she might be interested.

Of course she was interested. The idea didn't even seem so farfetched any more by the time she was introduced to Pete Wellesley. Nic's friend made Zanna think of a pirate, with his dreadlocked hair and a ring through one ear. With his easy smile and dancing eyes, it was impossible not to like him.

He had nothing like the controlled, bad-boy biker vibe that Nic had exuded at first sight but the combination of the two personalities was a force to be reckoned with. Pete's hint of mischief balanced Nic's intensity. Nic's attention to detail focused Pete's enthusiasm. She felt safe with Nic and inspired by Pete. They were both so confident and focused on the job at hand and they both seemed experts in their fields.

'We went through architectural school in London together,' Nic told her. 'And we both did a course on building heritage conservation. Pete took it further and did the thesis for his master's on relocation.'

'Did you do a thesis, too?' Zanna added a jar of olives and some cheese to the array of food she'd put together for a picnic-style lunch in the courtyard garden.

'His was on how to make money,' Pete told her.

'It was about blending modern architecture to the immediate physical environment,' Nic corrected.

'AKA how to make money.' Pete raised the bottle of beer he was holding in a toast. 'And good on you, mate. You do what you do very well.'

Zanna frowned. 'I thought you were an expert in *old* houses.'

The two men exchanged a glance. Then Nic caught Zanna's questioning gaze.

'My career has been all about developing luxury international coastal resorts and boutique hotels in the last few years but this is a special project,' he said.

His eyes added another message. That it was more than special. That he was completely invested in it because it was about someone he loved.

Her breath caught—held by the wave of emotion that swept through her. How long did it normally take two people to fall in love? If it happened this fast, did that make it an illusion?

A dream that she would have to wake up from?

The dream of saving her house might have taken an unexpected twist but, as the day wore on, it began to seem more and more possible.

'Turn of the century, you said?' With lunch and the introductory process complete, Pete had thrown himself into a thorough examination of the house, which had involved taking a lot of photographs and measurements. Having spent most of the afternoon exploring every inch, inside and out, they were finally back in the kitchen, sitting around the table as Pete entered data into his computer program. 'Do you know the exact year?'

Zanna shook her head. 'Nic seemed to think it was later than 1900 because of the Marseilles tiles. Does it matter?'

'Building styles varied a bit. If platform framing was used, which I expect it was, it means that the walls for each floor were framed separately above and below the first-floor joists. That makes it much easier to separate the floors for removal.'

Nerves kicked in again at that point. Alarm bells, even. 'I still can't believe you can chop a house up without doing enormous damage somewhere along the line.' There would be no going back if she agreed to this. No way to repair the damage if it turned out to be a mistake.

'But you saw the pictures of Pete's recent projects over lunch,' Nic reminded her, gesturing towards the tablet computer that was the only equipment Pete had brought with him other than a laser device for taking measurements. 'Even blowing up the images you couldn't tell where they'd been put back together.'

'This is a big house,' Pete said. 'It would need to go into six or maybe eight pieces. The only thing I can say for certain will get damaged are the roof tiles but you would have been looking at a replacement roof within a few years anyway.'

'That's true. There's been a leak in one of the spare bedrooms recently.' And they would never be able to afford a new roof so the damage would only accelerate.

'Slate would look good,' Nic suggested. 'Even better than the tiles.'

'It's wider than eighteen metres,' Pete continued, 'so it would need cutting twice. Where we cut depends on where the load-bearing walls are inside and any particular features that need protecting. Like the staircase.'

'And the turret,' Nic put in. 'That's got to be protected.'

'We'd remove that separately.' Pete was still tapping notes into his computer. 'Take it off with a crane. We'd separate the top storey. The ceiling of the ground floor stays with the floor of the upper storey so we'd have to put in bracing beams to hold the shape of the lower rooms together.' He stared at the screen for a long moment and then looked up to flash a grin at Zanna. 'It's doable,' he pronounced. 'And I have to say I'd relish the challenge. But you're lucky that those trees have been killed.'

Lucky? Was he serious?

'Those trees are hundreds of years old. Protected. There's nothing lucky about losing them.'

Pete raised an eyebrow in Nic's direction before turning towards Zanna. 'If they were still healthy there'd be no way you'd be allowed to take them down, and without taking them down there'd be no way of moving the house because of the high-rises around it and the big trees in the park.' He turned back to Nic. 'Are you going to give me another ride on that shiny toy you've hired and take me out to see the potential site for relocation? They're the last boxes I need to fill to get an estimate of costs.'

And then it would be a done deal.

'Sure.' Nic looked as though he was on the point of high-fiving Pete. 'And then I can drop you back at the airport. You okay with that, Zanna? I'll be a couple of hours.' He got to his feet, heading towards where he'd left the bike helmets on the floor near the French doors.

'No.' Zanna was surprised to hear the word coming out of her mouth but not nearly as startled as the two men looked.

'No,' she repeated, more firmly. 'I don't think I am okay with any of this.'

An awkward silence fell as Nic met her gaze. And then another significant glance passed between the men.

'How 'bout I meet you outside?' Pete suggested quietly.

A single nod and then they were alone.

'What's going on, Zanna?' Nic was careful not to sound impatient. 'I thought you were on board. That you liked the idea.'

It had felt like a done deal, in fact. The estimate of costs was not important. Nic was more than prepared to cover whatever it was going to cost. The goalposts were in sight and he could smell success.

'It's all happening too fast. I haven't had a chance to think about it properly, let alone talk to Maggie. I feel like I'm being railroaded. Bullied, even… And I made a promise to myself that I would never let that happen again.'

What on earth was she talking about?

'What do you mean…*again*? I'm not trying to railroad you. Quite the opposite. I didn't even talk about it last night because I wanted to give you time to think about it without feeling pressured, but…' He ran his fingers through his hair. It was a risk but if he didn't push things here, there was a real danger of all the work he'd done so far being for nothing. 'There *is* a time limit. You need my help and I can't be here much longer. We've only a few days to get it all sorted.'

'I wasn't talking about you.'

Something in Zanna's eyes gave Nic that feeling of wanting to protect her again. Of wanting to make everything all right. For a heartbeat it was actually stronger than what he wanted for himself.

Long enough for him to hold her gaze and close the gap between them. To take her hands and hold them.

'So tell me who you are talking about. Trust me, Zanna.' She wouldn't be disappointed if she did. He'd make sure of that. 'Please.'

'That's the problem,' she whispered. 'Trust…'

Nic knew that Pete was waiting for him outside beside the motorbike. Probably impatient to get going and get this project kicked into some real action. As impatient as he was himself.

But this was important.

Vital, in fact.

He led Zanna towards the table and invited her to sit. He was ready to listen and solve any problem that was about to make an appearance. He was good at that. Not that Zanna seemed in a hurry to get to the point.

'I never thought I could make a living out of my art,' she told him. 'It was a dream that seemed too good to believe in. I didn't even go to art school for years. I did a degree in art conservation first. I imagined myself working in a museum and getting up close and personal with the work of famous artists.'

Nic made an encouraging noise.

'But the more time I spent around art, the more I loved doing my own work. It was my best friend, Brie, who persuaded me to do a postgraduate art degree in London, and Maggie took out another mortgage on the house to pay for it. She'd always believed in me, she said, and when I was rich and famous I could pay her back.'

Nick waited, slotting away the information that there was more than one mortgage on the house. No problem. He could make the offer even more attractive.

'Brie came to London with me. She scored a job in a big gallery and that was how I met Simon. Brie started a campaign to get him interested in me. He was a big wheel in the European art scene and the careers of artists he picked as up and coming really took off.'

Nic didn't like the way she closed her eyes and took a deep breath. He had the feeling that this Simon was important to Zanna and he didn't like that. Good grief, was that unpleasant prickle of sensation jealousy?

'Brie's campaign worked a treat,' Zanna said. 'He chose me for more than just my art. We were living together in a matter of weeks. Talking about getting married.'

Yep. It was jealousy.

'He really wanted to help my career but he said that the kind of work I did—the flowers and cats and everything—was craft more than art. I needed to try something more contemporary. Edgier.'

Nic snorted. The man was an idiot. Had he not really looked at Zanna's paintings? Could he not appreciate how they could make people feel? Not that he knew anything much about art but surely the emotional impact was what mattered?

'It didn't feel right,' Zanna continued quietly. 'But this was my best friend and my fiancé who were trying to persuade me and I was in love so, of course, I trusted them. I let them push me in a direction I would never have chosen for myself and they pushed hard. I spent months working on a collection for an exhibition. Huge paintings. I must have gone to every old cemetery in London to choose the gravestones I based the work around.'

'Gravestones?' Nic's jaw dropped. 'You had a theme of death in your work?'

'Pretty much.' Zanna shrugged. 'It was edgy. Dark. Art, not craft.'

Nic thought of the rich colours in Zanna's paintings. The warmth. The feeling of movement and life captured in those sketches of the cats.

'They didn't know you very well, did they?'

Zanna's breath came out in a huff. 'Maybe they knew me very well. Maybe the campaign had never been about getting my career as an artist off the ground.' She shook her head. 'I'm not sure I really believe they set out to destroy me. Maybe it was a game that took on a life of its own. Or maybe it came from a subconscious need to get me out of the way. Anyway—' her voice became harsh '—it worked. They got what they wanted out of it.'

'Which was?'

'Each other, of course. The humiliation of the awful reviews my exhibition got was only part of it. I went home after a particularly horrible day to find Simon and Brie in bed together.'

'Merde...' Nic wanted to find this Simon idiot and ruin him. The way he'd tried to ruin Zanna. 'So that was why you left London?'

She nodded. 'I came home to the one person I knew I could trust absolutely. To the place I felt safe.'

Her refuge. He'd known there was something huge behind her use of that particular word. It had been that glimpse of her vulnerability that had touched something unexpected deep within him. Had been the catalyst for everything that had filled the time they'd had together since.

And he was expecting her to pick that refuge up and shake it in the hope of keeping something so precious safe. He was asking her to trust him when he wasn't even being entirely honest with her.

He could see something in himself in that moment that he wasn't proud of and the sensation was even more unpleasant than any twinge of jealousy. He'd had moments in his life when he'd hated himself and this took him back to feeling inadequate. Totally powerless. Angry instead of sad that he was losing something—no, some*one*—precious to him.

He tightened his grip on Zanna's hands. Held her gaze. If he could put this right, he might know that it was possible to do more than let her know it was okay to trust someone. He might discover that it was possible to be a better person himself and escape from a legacy that he'd thought would always haunt him. But he'd gotten in so deep—how could he even start to fix things without doing more damage? If Zanna thought she had misplaced her trust again, would she hide behind a protective barrier for the rest of her life?

She deserved better than that. How could you truly love someone if complete trust was missing? She deserved the chance to give her love without reservation and the man who was lucky enough to win that love deserved to know all of Zanna because she was so special. Unique.

'I need to take Pete out to see the land,' he said slowly. 'But that doesn't mean I'm trying to push you in a direction you don't want to go. If you decide you don't want to do this, that's fine.'

He meant every word. He might have the power to make sure he got what he wanted here but if it was at the expense of abusing the trust he was asking Zanna to put in him then he would back off. He would find another way to create a memorial to his parents.

Zanna nodded. 'I'll try and get hold of Maggie and talk to her about this. See how she feels.'

The timing of Maggie's phone call couldn't have been better.

Nic had been gone for more than two hours and Zanna had been pacing, her mind darting back and forth over a confusing spectrum.

Nic was nothing like Simon. He wasn't trying to change her into someone she wasn't. He was offering to help secure the place where she was herself most of all. He *got* her work. Unconditionally. It didn't matter a damn to him if the people who knew about art dismissed it as craft.

If she went ahead with this new plan, she would have a studio in an idyllic location that would be safe to live in for ever. With a business that could support her even if she never had the courage to try selling her work.

And he'd been right. He wasn't pushing her into agreeing with his idea. He'd backed off completely to give her space to think about it. Filled that space with the reassurance that it was safe to trust him, in fact.

To love him?

He wasn't Simon and he'd made her feel amazing things again. She would only hurt herself if she let Simon's legacy destroy something this beautiful and, if she let that happen this time, she could be setting a precedent that meant she would never truly trust anyone again.

She wanted it to happen. Both the house relocation and possibly finding a relationship that was strong enough to overcome the obvious logistical problems like living on different sides of the world, but it was terrifying to be getting this close when so much could go wrong.

What if Nic didn't feel the same way about what they'd found with each other?

What if Pete had found something about the potential site that was going to make it not doable or too expensive?

What if Maggie flatly refused to entertain the idea of such a radical sideways move to save the house?

Maybe it wasn't surprising that she burst into tears the moment she heard her aunt's voice on the phone.

Of course Maggie knew exactly the right things to say until Zanna calmed down enough to start talking. And then she listened without interrupting, other than to encourage her, as Zanna poured out everything she needed to say. Her voice was choked with tears when she told her aunt about the trees and it wobbled when she relayed the information that the council's decision to enforce the sale could be imminent.

'But Pete says it's lucky the trees have been killed,' she finished, 'because otherwise we couldn't even think about shifting it. And Nic says that the spirit of the house is about the people, not the place it's sitting, but…this is so huge, Maggie. How do I know that I can trust him?'

'You need to listen to your heart, darling. It will tell you all you need to know. You had your doubts about Simon right from the start, didn't you? You couldn't understand why he'd chosen you. You felt you had to change to deserve him. He's the one who needed to change. He didn't deserve *you*.'

A smile tugged at Zanna's lips for the first time in this conversation. Nic didn't want her to change. He wanted her to be safe to be herself. This whole plan was about protecting the things that were most important to her.

Her smile grew. 'Oh, Maggie—you should see the land that he's found for sale. It's just out of town and there's a lake and a forest and—and it's all *so* gorgeous. There's an old stable block that could become the shop and tea rooms. You'd love it.'

'*You* love it, darling, and that's all that matters.'

'It's not just up to me. This was your house long before I came to share it. It's your business. This has to be your decision and whatever you decide, I'll support you, you know that.'

'I know. So don't be upset when I tell you what I've decided, will you?'

A prickle of fear sent a shock wave down Zanna's spine. She was going to veto the project?

'I've decided to stay here,' Maggie said softly. 'Dimitry's asked me to marry him.'

'*What?* Oh, my God…' Zanna had to back up against the wall to find some support and she still found herself sinking to a crouch. '*Maggie…* You've only just met him. You can't possibly be sure about something that huge.'

'Oh, darling…' There was laughter in her aunt's voice. 'I've waited my whole life to find this. Do you think I didn't recognise it instantly? The only thing I wasn't sure of was whether Dimitry felt the same way. When it's right, you just know… Well, I did anyway. I have had a lot of practice in reading people.'

'Oh…' Zanna was closer to tears now than she had been in talking about the trees. A roller-coaster of emotions was going at full speed in her head and her heart. Happiness that Maggie had found the love of her life. Sadness that they were going to be living so far apart and that the closeness of their relationship would inevitably change. Jealousy, even, that there was someone else who would be Maggie's first priority. And running beneath all those dips and swoops were the rails of something that felt like…hope?

That Maggie was right? That there were no rules about how long it should take to know if you'd met the love of your life?

That what she'd found with Nic could be *real…*

'I gave you power of attorney, my love, and now I'm giving you more than that. The house is yours to do whatever you want to do with it. All I ask is that you take care of those cats of ours and keep the things you'll know I want to come back for safe. Now...' Even on the end of a phone line, half a world away and without the benefit of the card ritual, Maggie seemed to be able to read her mind. 'Tell me all about this Nic.'

Zanna was smiling again. 'He's French, Maggie. His full name is Dominic Brabant...'

'Brabant?' Maggie sounded startled. 'Where have I heard that name before? Oh, no...it couldn't be... Or maybe it could...'

'Here it is.' Nic pulled the folded sheet of paper from an inside pocket of his leather jacket. 'A formal estimate of the cost of shifting the house and repositioning it and a pretty generous estimate of what we think the costs of complete renovation would be.'

Was it his imagination or was Zanna sitting curiously still at the kitchen table, her fingers resting gently around the stem of a crystal glass? An open bottle of wine was beside the flickering candelabra, an empty glass beside it. Nic raised an eyebrow as he shed his jacket and her half-smile was an invitation so he poured himself a glass and sat down. He unfolded the sheet of paper and pushed it closer to Zanna.

'We got it printed out at the business centre in the airport lounge. And I've added the asking price of the land as well. See?'

'Good grief.' Zanna touched the paper as if she couldn't believe what she was seeing. 'That's nearly two million dollars.'

Nic covered her hand with his own. 'That's why I'm going to offer you three million for this property.'

This was the first step in putting things right. To make sure that Zanna understood that the dream solution he had presented was possible. That life would be secure in the future for both herself and the aunt she clearly adored.

The next step would be some honesty.

The silence that followed was unnerving. So was the way Zanna was looking at him. The way she slid her hand out from beneath his so very carefully. As if he'd done something unforgiveable.

'Why, Nic?'

'What do you mean?'

'Why would you offer me so much? The last registered valuation for this place was way less than half of that. The last offer Prime Property came up with was only six hundred thousand. Why do *you* want it so much?'

There was something in her tone that told him the game was up. That the opportunity to be voluntarily honest had been lost. His mouth suddenly dry, Nic took a long swallow of his wine.

'I've been talking to Maggie,' Zanna told him.

'Oh… She's not happy about the idea, then?'

The shake of Zanna's head dismissed his response as irrelevant. 'Was your mother's name Elise?'

CHAPTER EIGHT

IF HE WAS SHOCKED, he was hiding it well.

There was, in fact, a softening in his eyes that looked curiously like joy.

'Maggie remembers her?'

It made it worse that Nic seemed happy to have been found out. It was rubbing salt into what felt like a very raw wound.

How could he? Just a breath after she'd bared her soul and told him about how devastating Simon and Brie's betrayal had been. How hard it was for her to trust anyone's motives.

He wasn't even considering how she might be feeling right now but maybe he'd realise if she kept talking. Surely the strain in her voice was obvious?

'She said she was very beautiful, with long dark hair, but she was very shy because she thought she didn't speak English very well. And she didn't need anyone else in her life, anyway, because she totally adored her husband.'

The way she could have adored Nic. Not that he had any idea that she'd been ready to give him her whole heart. Her trust.

She couldn't go there now. No way.

Stupidly, though, her heart hadn't caught up with what her head was telling her in no uncertain terms.

And Nic was oblivious. He was hanging onto every word she spoke. This was important to him. Far more important than picking up on the sense of betrayal Zanna was fighting with because he hadn't told her about any of it.

It was a real effort to keep her voice steady. 'She remembers that she was a brilliant musician and she gave piano lessons to local children. She could sing beautifully too and your father played the guitar and she would hear them at night, singing French love songs in the garden.'

And how easy would it have been to hear that when it was coming from the garden right next door? From the people who'd lived in one of the small cottages that had been removed to make the public park.

His eyes were so dark. They caught the candlelight just then. Because of the moisture of unshed tears? The accusation that had unmistakeably laced her last words seemed to have gone as undetected as how upset she was.

'They had a baby they called Dommi. Maggie said she'd never seen such a happy little family.'

He looked away from her and his mouth tightened. Was it painful to hear this?

Good. Why should she be the only one suffering here?

'You said you were taken back to France when you were six years old.'

A single nod but Nic didn't say anything.

'You didn't tell me it was because your mother got evicted from her cottage because she couldn't manage her rent. That your father had been killed in a tragic accident at his work a year or more before that.'

'No.' The words were raw. 'I didn't tell you that.'

Her heart made her want to reach out and touch him because she knew he needed comfort. Her head made her throw an even bigger verbal spear.

'It's a bit of a coincidence that the historical protection society sent you to evaluate this house, isn't it?'

There was an accusation in her tone that grated. Zanna had no idea what fragile ground she was treading on here. How intrusive it felt to let someone else into this part of his life. To trust someone enough to share any of this story. And it was being forced on him before he was ready.

There was anger to be found there. Nobody had managed to force him to do anything once he'd been old enough to gain control of his own life.

But she knew already. The protective walls around that hidden place had been breached.

And she had trusted him, hadn't she? She'd opened her heart and shared the pain of the life she'd thought she'd had in London imploding.

Dommi. He hadn't heard that name since he was twelve years old and his mother had died. He'd become Dominic with the formalities of going into care and he'd chosen Nic when he was sixteen and found work that enabled him to become independent. To take control and steer his life towards a place where he'd never have to feel that kind of pain any more.

Nobody knew. Not even Pete—his closest friend—knew more than sketchy details of his background. And Pete had no idea why he'd decided to take on this project, although he'd guessed straight off that he'd been hiding something.

'I wasn't sent here to evaluate the house. I never told you that.'

'You knew that was what I thought. You didn't tell me the truth.'

Nic closed his eyes. 'No.'

This was it. The destruction of trust. He wasn't going to come out of this feeling like a better person. He was going to think less of himself. How on earth had this happened? He'd spent so many years building up defences against precisely this and somehow this woman had slipped under his skin and had the power to leave him unprotected and vulnerable.

'Why not, Nic?' The faint wobble in her words cut straight through his heart. 'Did you think I wouldn't understand?'

His eyes snapped open. Was it possible that she *did* understand? That she could forgive him for the deception?

She'd been through her own childhood trauma, hadn't she? She'd been lucky to have found a loving home so she couldn't know how soul destroying it was to be handed around like an unwanted parcel, but she did know what it was like to lose your parents.

'Do you remember what it was like when your parents were killed, Zanna? How you felt?'

She nodded slowly. 'It was like the world had ended. I was lost and very, very frightened.'

'It was like that for my mother and me when Papa was killed. And my world *had* ended as I'd known it. Maman couldn't get over it. She got sick. The children who came for lessons went away. She took me back to her home country but there was no way she could find work. She got really sick, with cancer that went undiagnosed until far too late. I think she wanted to die, so that she could be with Papa again.'

'Oh...*Nic...*' Zanna could hear the bewildered child behind those words. Feel the pain of thinking you couldn't make things better. That you weren't good enough or something. Her heart was definitely winning the battle over her head now and the urge to comfort was getting overwhelming. Being fuelled by an urge to forgive? 'How old were you when she died?'

'Twelve.'

'So you got taken into care?'

His nod was terse. He wasn't going to talk about those years. Ever.

'I'd already learned to stop remembering when life had been good because it only made things worse. I got very, very good at it. I hadn't even thought about any of it for years and years. Until I saw this house again. The next-door house that had the scary lady living in it.'

That brought a wry smile to Zanna's lips. 'Yeah... I thought she was pretty scary at first, too. Larger than life, that's for sure. Nothing like anybody I'd ever known.'

Zanna was nothing like anybody Nic had ever known. After watching the play of emotions on her face he had to focus again on what he needed to say.

'I did come to New Zealand for an entirely different reason,' he admitted, 'and the memories were hard to handle because I hadn't expected them. I'm ready now. To remember.' He swallowed hard. 'To honour those memories.' He met Zanna's gaze. 'I couldn't share them. They were too raw. Too personal. And...I didn't know you.'

'But you do now.'

'I do.' Her eyes were so soft. He hadn't seen an expression like that since…since his mother had told him how much she loved him. The squeeze in his chest was so painful he had to look away.

'Would you have told me—if I hadn't found out?'

'I was going to tell you tonight. I couldn't *not* tell you. Not after you told me about what happened in London. I…don't want to hurt you, Zanna.'

He was starting to gain the skill of reading her. He could see the flicker in her eyes that told him she could hear the truth in his words. The softening of something in her face that let him know that trust might have been bruised but it was still intact. Just.

He could certainly feel the tension ebbing rapidly.

'What do you want to do to honour those memories? Is that why you want to buy this property?'

'Yes.' Nic took a deep breath and then he told her about the vision for the music school. How it would sit beside the river and the park and look like it was meant to be there. How the sound of music would drift across the tiny patch of the earth where his parents had been so happy. Where he'd been so happy. He wanted to put a beautiful bench seat in the park with their names on it so that people could sit and listen to the music. He told her about the gallery he wanted to put in the foyer of the school to honour Rata House.

He wasn't sure at what point he'd taken hold of Zanna's hands. Or maybe she'd taken hold of his. It didn't matter. She listened to every word and there were tears on her cheeks when he finally stopped talking.

'That's so beautiful, Nic. We were fighting so hard to save this house partly because we knew that if it went in the future when we weren't here, something horrible might take its place—like a huge hotel or another apartment block like next door. But your music school…that's exactly what should be here. Oh, Maggie will love that.' A smile broke through the tears. 'Maybe fate kept us fighting just so that it would be here for you.'

It was hard to swallow past the lump in his throat. Hard to breathe against the constriction in his chest. And Nic had to blink hard to clear the prickle behind his eyes.

She *did* understand.

And he knew he could love her for that.

This was a gift. Did it even matter that he hadn't told her about owning the apartment block?

Yes, his head said. It could change everything.

No, his heart said. It could change everything.

Trust would not survive a second blow. Not before it had had time to get stronger. Maybe he should have told her that was what had brought him here in the first place instead of clouding it with a vague reference to an entirely different reason. If she'd asked what that reason had been, he would have told her.

But it was too late now. Saying anything else might dilute this incredible feeling of being understood. Of having someone beside him. Sharing his dream because she understood exactly why it was so important.

Or was it too late? If she understood as well as she seemed to, she would see how the purchase of the apartment block had been the catalyst for all of this and it could be dismissed along with the deception of having let her assume he'd come onto her property on behalf of the city council.

But there was a new light in Zanna's eyes now. Excitement.

'How soon can we start the ball rolling?'

'We can get the papers drawn up on Monday.' How much easier was it to buy into that excitement and silence the argument going on between his head and his heart? 'No…I've got legal contacts. Someone will be happy to work on a Sunday if they get paid well enough.'

'I'll call our solicitor,' Zanna said. 'Keith Watson. We've known him for years and years and he's helped us a lot. Given us free advice every time we've faced trouble from the council or needed to know how to handle harassment from the Scallions. He loves this house. He'll be thrilled to know it's going to be reborn.'

'Once the agreement for sale and purchase is finalised, we can give Pete the green light. If we make an immediate possession date, we can get started as soon as you're ready.'

'What am I going to do with all the stuff in the house and shop? It'll all have to come out for the removal process.'

'We'll find a storage facility. Get packers in.'

But Zanna shook her head. 'I'll need to sort everything. Maggie's going to want a lot of her things and they're precious. Like those antique instruments. I'd want to pack and shift those myself to make sure they're safe. I promised her I'd keep them safe.'

'We'll make sure they are.' The excitement was gaining force. Bubbling between them—the future so bright with the potential for amazing things to happen.

The conviction that he could do anything with Zanna by his side took Nic by surprise. He'd walked alone for ever and this feeling of shared anticipation was something new. It felt like he'd put a magnifying glass on the satisfaction he'd always felt when a new challenge was falling into place. How much greater would the joy be when it was complete?

He wanted Zanna by his side, then, too. He wanted to open the door of her restored house to take her for a tour. He wanted her holding his hand as they cut the ribbon for the opening of the Brabant Music Academy.

He couldn't imagine *not* wanting Zanna.

It was as simple as that.

And he felt like he was looking into a reflection of how he was feeling as he gazed into Zanna's eyes.

Conversation had died. Tomorrow would be soon enough to start talking through the thousands of details. Tonight was for celebrating what was going to be achieved.

Together.

Words wouldn't be enough, anyway. There was only one way that Nic could show Zanna how much it meant to him to have someone sharing this part of his soul.

Zanna couldn't tell where her body left off and Nic's started as he rose from the table to lead her upstairs. Maybe that was because she had started to move at exactly the same moment, with exactly the same destination in mind.

Any sense of betrayal had long since been extinguished. Of course he'd been unable to let a stranger into a place that he'd kept hidden for so long, even to himself. How could she blame him for taking an opportunity to protect that privacy when she'd made it so easy?

But he'd invited her in now.

He trusted her.

Maybe, this time, she could really trust her own instincts. Trust *him*. Trust the inherited wisdom that generations of seers had given Maggie.

When it was right, you just *knew*.

CHAPTER NINE

THE NEXT FEW DAYS passed in a blur.

Looking back, Zanna knew she would remember only bits of it but they were memories that she would always treasure.

The night together after he'd told her so much about what had made him into the person he was. How being invited into such a personal space had made her love him so much more.

The way Nic had looked when the contract had been signed and that first, major step had been taken. Not that she'd agreed to be paid so much more than the property was worth. Two million was enough. He could put the rest into the music school.

The surprise of discovering how well Nic could play a guitar when they were packing up Maggie's old instruments. Listening to him singing her a French love song late at night, out in the courtyard, with the chiminea and candelabra providing all the warmth and light they could need.

Knowing that this was where she always needed to be. By Nic's side.

She'd started some packing in the shop now, too. Boxes of stock were being sent to join others in the storage facility they'd hired. There was a notice on the door explaining why Spellbound would have to close in the near future but she was happy to assure customers that the business would start again before too long in an even better place.

The cats were unsettled by all the unusual activity and seemed to be always underfoot, seeking reassurance.

'It's all okay,' Zanna kept telling them. 'I know it's a worry but you guys are going to be so happy in the country. There'll be trees to climb and lots of mice to catch. You probably won't even want your tinned food any more.'

They didn't seem to want it very much at the moment. On Tuesday night, Zanna tapped the spoon against the bowl but there was no streak of black coming from any direction.

'Where are they?'

Nic glanced up from his laptop. After meetings that morning with the council planning department to apply for various permits and checking out storage facilities, he'd started preliminary plans for the music school and had been absorbed for the rest of the afternoon while Zanna had been busy in the shop. 'I haven't seen them for hours. Not even Merlin.'

'That's weird. I'd better check that I didn't lock them in the shop by mistake. They were hanging around when I was packing in there earlier.'

The cats had, indeed, been accidentally locked in the shop. Maybe they'd been asleep on the pile of clothing behind the stack of boxes Zanna had filled that day. It was Merlin who jumped into her arms as she opened the door but Marmite and Mystic glued themselves to her ankles, competing for attention with plaintive cries of having been imprisoned.

Zanna was laughing as she tried to get down the steps without the cats tripping her up but the laughter died the moment she felt the hairs on the back of her neck prickle.

She wasn't alone.

The shop was dark and empty behind her. The front door of the house was open not far away but Nic was in the kitchen at the back and probably too far away and too focused on what he was doing to hear her even if she screamed.

Maybe she was imagining things. The light of the day was almost gone and the wind had picked up so the shadows cast by the massive, dying trees and the sound of creaking branches was spooky.

Then she looked beyond the trees. The streetlights would come on at any moment now and, when they did, the figure standing beside the lamppost just outside the gate would be instantly obvious.

A male figure. Just standing there. Even without being able to see him clearly, she knew he was staring at the house.

At her.

A tourist out for a walk, she told herself. Someone had stopped to look at the curiosity the house had become.

Except that a tourist wouldn't feel like such a threat. They wouldn't be standing with such…nonchalance? And they certainly wouldn't emit a sound like low laughter. Merlin stiffened in her arms and responded with a hiss.

'Evening, Miss Zelensky.' He made her name sound like an insult. 'How's it going?'

The cats at her feet were gone in a streak, heading

for the safety of the house. Merlin's claws dug painfully into Zanna's arms as he launched himself in the wake of his siblings. Following them herself might have been a sensible option but it wasn't the way she responded to a threat. Instead, she became very still. Centring herself and gathering her strength.

'Blake. What are you doing here?'

'Happened to be in town. Just wanted a look.'

'You've looked. You can go now.'

The man Maggie had always referred to as the junior scorpion took a step closer. The rusty, wrought-iron gate was permanently ajar. Another step and he would be on the brick pathway.

'There's nothing here for you. The property's sold.' She couldn't help the note of satisfaction that coated her words. 'To someone else.'

'I know.'

Zanna felt that prickle in her spine again. A premonition of danger. She tried to shake it off. Prime Property couldn't threaten them any longer. Or was that why Blake was here? Was he angry that they'd lost their long battle?

He didn't seem angry. There was a smugness in those words.

'It's none of your business.'

He laughed again. 'You sure about that?' He turned, as if intending to walk away. 'Tell Nic I'll give him a call tomorrow. We need to talk.'

The prickle turned into a chill that sent ice into Zanna's veins. This time it was her moving to narrow the gap between them.

'Why would I do that? What makes you think he would want to have anything to do with the likes of you?'

Blake turned back. She could see the gleam of his teeth as he smiled.

'We've been partners for years, sweetheart. Dad and I were only too delighted to get rid of having to deal with you and your aunt and obviously he managed to do what we couldn't. In record time, too. What was so attractive about what he had to offer, Suzanna?' The tone was a sneer. 'As if I couldn't guess.'

'I don't believe you. Get out, Blake. I don't ever want to see you or your father again. Set foot on this property and I'll call the police. You could still be charged with malicious damage after what you did to our trees.'

'We could sue you for malicious damage right back. You've got no idea of the grief you've caused us, sweetheart. It's lucky that the heart attack didn't kill Dad. At least he'll get the pleasure of seeing you gone. Of seeing this house knocked flat.' He took another long glance upwards. 'Good riddance, I say. Good on you, Nic.'

This time when he turned he kept moving. The streetlights came on in time for Zanna to see his silhouette fade as he walked past the apartment block.

No. She couldn't believe that Nic would be in partnership with the Scallions. He would tell her how ridiculous the very idea was as soon as he heard about it. She started walking towards the front door of the house but then stopped.

It made sense.

Nic had said that his career was usually about luxury international coastal resorts—exactly the kind of developments that Prime Property was famous for.

He had hidden his connection to the property from the moment he'd walked in. Sure, she knew the story about his background was true, thanks to Maggie, but didn't that make it worse? He had come here with a single purpose in mind and perhaps the motive of knowing even a hint of association with Prime Property would have made him unwelcome to set foot in the house had been stronger than a desire to keep his background private.

And he'd gone so much further than merely setting foot in her house...

Oh...*God*...

Had she been played? Sucked into going in a direction she'd never intended? The way Simon and Brie had persuaded her to change her art? What if she was heading for an even bigger fall that she'd never be able to come back from? That she'd trusted someone enough to reveal her humiliation only to find that history was repeating itself?

Her mind raced on to imagine the worst. What if it turned out that the house fell apart when they tried to shift it? It would only be her loss, wouldn't it? They'd still have their patch of land. *Two* patches of land. Enough for the biggest hotel in town, and maybe that was the real agenda. Maybe Nic's connection to this property had just been a fortunate coincidence. That the music school would be deemed uneconomic or something before it got past the planning stage.

No. The things Nic had told her were true. They'd come straight from his heart. She *believed* him.

She'd believed Simon, too.

Maybe her instincts couldn't be trusted.

Or maybe she'd been ignoring the warnings those instincts had issued. She could hear an echo of his voice. Of hers as well, during that card reading.

'Sometimes you have to let go of an old life in order to take the opportunity of a new and fulfilling one.'

'Something I've always lived by... Do you?*'*

There had been a moment of warning she hadn't ignored, even then.

He may not be who he seems to be. Take care...

It was Nic who'd spotted the holes in the trees.

And who just happened to have a mate who specialised in relocating old houses. She'd noticed those odd glances between the two men that day, hadn't she?

But it had all worked, hadn't it? She'd signed legal contracts. No wonder Blake had sounded so smug.

If only Maggie was here, Zanna thought desperately. She felt so alone. She could be on the point of losing everything. Losing the house would be bad enough but she had the horrible feeling she was about to lose Nic as well.

Merlin jumped onto Nic's lap but he pushed him off as the tail cut his view of the computer screen in half. Offended, the cat started washing himself but Nic didn't notice. He'd finally got the line just right. The curve of the building as it echoed the line of the river. The software program he was using allowed him to layer the plan on top of the aerial photographs of the area that he'd already removed both Rata House and the apartment block from. He could circle it now and get an idea of how it sat from both the street side and the river side.

He heard Zanna finally come back but still didn't turn his head.

'Come and look at this. I think I've nailed it.'

It was the silence that finally broke his concentration. Nothing like the quiet serenity that Zanna was capable of generating sometimes. This was a heavy silence. Ominous. When he looked up and saw her face, he uttered a low oath.

'What's wrong? What's happened?'

Had one of the cats been run over or something? Merlin was sitting nearby, licking a paw and then scraping it over his face. And, yes…there were two cats still engrossed in eating.

Had she had some bad news about her aunt? Surely someone must have died to make her look like that. So shocked. Drained of any vestige of colour.

'Are you part of Prime Property, Nic?' Her voice was flat. 'A partner?'

'No.' His chair scraped on the wooden floor as he pushed it back to get to his feet. 'Hell, no…' He started to walk towards Zanna but she held her hand up and it felt like he'd hit a force field. He stopped in his tracks.

'I just found Blake Scallion standing outside the gate. He said he'd call you tomorrow because you *needed to talk.*' He could see Zanna's throat move as she swallowed. '*He* said you'd been partners for years. I didn't believe him but then I thought…it could be true. Maybe you had been sent to *deal* with the little problem that Maggie and I represented.'

'I'm not a partner of Prime Property. Yes, I've worked with them. They've used my designs to develop coastal resorts. The way other property development companies use my expertise all over the world for all sorts of projects. That was why I was in New Zealand in the first place. They've bought a huge block of land on the Hibiscus Coast and they want me on board to get another resort off the ground.'

This was the explanation he should have given her long ago but it was too late now. Way too late.

'But you've bought this property.' Zanna's expression was frozen. She wasn't prepared to believe anything he was going to say to try and explain. 'The one that Prime Property's been trying to get hold of for the last ten years. They still own the one next door. Another *coincidence*?'

'They don't own next door any more. I couldn't have started the project for the music school unless I had both properties.'

'So *you* own the apartment block now?' A wash of colour stained Zanna's cheeks. Anger…? Or maybe it was relief. He could defuse this whole situation if he took the opportunity she was offering and let her believe that he'd approached the Scallions to sell the apartment block only after he'd purchased Rata House. 'When did you buy that—or is that why Blake wants to talk to you tomorrow?'

Nic closed his eyes. Deception by omission was one thing. An outright lie was unacceptable. Yes, telling the truth could change everything but he had no choice. And maybe he needed a leap of faith. It would only be a glimmer of hope but she might understand—the way she seemed to have understood everything else about him. He opened his eyes.

'I bought the apartment block ten days ago. Before I came here.'

He had to let the silence extend as Zanna processed what he'd said. He could feel his heart thumping and it skipped a beat completely when she finally spoke again because her voice sounded so tightly controlled. Cold.

'So you came here knowing that you couldn't go ahead with your plans unless you persuaded me to sell?'

He didn't need to say anything. She could see the truth in his eyes.

And it hurt so much more than she'd tried to prepare herself for.

'Is there really going to be a music school, Nic, or was that part of the grand plan? Get me on side with the sob story of your unhappy childhood? Pete said you're good at making money. Wouldn't a really *big* apartment block or a hotel or something be more in your line of work?'

She could see that her accusation had hit home but the flash of shock in his face was quickly masked. A barrier was going up between them. A huge, impenetrable barrier.

That hurt, too.

A *sob story*? Had he really thought she understood? He'd let her into the most private part of his soul and she was dismissing it as being some sort of manipulative device.

Nic could feel his head taking over completely from his heart. Putting him in a professional mode. This was what he'd come here for, wasn't it? A business deal. And he'd succeeded. It should be enough.

Clearly, it would have to be enough.

'You're getting what you wanted out of it, aren't you? Yes, I wanted the land but when I met you and saw how you felt about the house I knew it shouldn't be simply demolished. You were right in wanting to save it but you wouldn't have won in the long run when you can't afford to even maintain it where it is. I came up with a solution that gave us both what we wanted. I made that solution possible. Do you think you could have done this without my contacts? Like Pete? Like the estate agent who told me about land that wasn't even on the market yet?'

'You were holding all the cards. You were hiding the truth. Did you just happen to spot those holes in the trees or did you already know they were there? Had you been in on those plans, too? *Years* ago?'

'No. I had no idea Prime Property had any interest in this place until I saw a file on Donald's desk two weeks ago. The picture of a house I could never forget. They have no idea why I wanted to take over the project. I haven't even told Pete what I've got in mind here. You're the only person who knows that. Knows why it matters.'

The only person who understood that he was chasing a memory. Trying to catch and preserve a fragment of how it had felt to be loved and safe. Surely she could remember how it had felt to be in each other's arms that night? That they were the only two people in the world who could share the pain of that particular loss and the joy of turning it into something meaningful?

Zanna couldn't miss the intensity of his words. She knew what Nic was trying to tap into—that shared vision of honouring both their pasts with the music school and its gallery. The trust he'd won from her by sharing his secrets.

But it wasn't going to work this time. Trust wasn't something you could keep breaking and then gluing back together. This time she was going to protect herself more effectively. And it wasn't a total disaster, was it? Maybe she wasn't going to lose the house. She might end up with that dream property in the green belt, with her house and the business intact and a place that could inspire her real work with her art.

Was that enough to make up for what she was definitely losing here?

That trust? The ability to love somebody with her entire heart and soul?

He'd come here with the same agenda that the Scallions had always had. To get her out so that they could have what they wanted. He'd lied to her. More than that…

Shame and anger curdled the grief of loss.

'Do you often have to sleep with potential sellers, Nic?' It was hard to force the words out because every one of them hurt. 'Get them to fall in love with you so that they'll be only too happy to fall into line?'

That shattered the barrier for a heartbeat. Good grief…had he really not had *any* idea how she felt about him?

Did he think she'd been playing some kind of game, too? *Acting?*

'Bit silly of me to persuade you to offer less, wasn't it?' Zanna finally broke the distance she'd held between them. She walked to the table and picked up the sheaf of papers that was her copy of the sale and agreement purchase. She ripped it in half.

She only had to lean a little to snap shut the lid of Nic's laptop.

'Game over,' she said calmly. 'Get out, Nic.'

And then she turned and walked out of the room.

Into the hallway beneath the sunflower painting, but she didn't let herself remember the way Nic's reaction to seeing it had made her feel. Had mattered so much.

She couldn't trust anything she felt any more and, as if demanding recognition, there were overwhelming emotions boiling up inside. The pain of betrayal. The grief of loss. The shame of being deceived. Broken love. All competing with a desperate desire not to believe any of them but to trust how she felt about Nic. Any one of them was powerful enough to make her shake like this.

She had to keep moving so she didn't sink into a quivering heap that Nic would have to step around on his way out of the house. She ran up the wide stairs and still she kept going. There was only one place she could go to find some sort of release from the storm. A refuge that would allow her to clear her head and start to think instead of being battered by this crashing emotional surf.

She slammed the door at the top of the spiral staircase behind her.

And then she locked it.

CHAPTER TEN

GUNNING THE ENGINE of the bike was a satisfying echo to the anger heating Nic's blood. Opening the throttle as soon as he escaped the city's speed limits and leaning into the blast of cold air finally cooled that heat enough for the shock waves to stop blasting him from all directions.

He was miles out of the city now. In a small town whose main street boasted a motel, a Chinese takeaway restaurant and a liquor store.

Perfect. A bed for the night, something to eat and a bottle of even halfway decent Scotch and he could sort this whole mess out. He could start defining exactly what was making him so damn angry and that was a very necessary first step before he decided what he was going to do next. Anger had no place in making rational decisions.

An hour or two later and being dismissed by Zanna Zelensky in the wake of her ripping up their contract was top of the list of what was making his blood boil.

The knee-jerk reaction was that *il n'avait pas d'importance*—it made no difference. It was only a copy of a legally binding contract and his solicitor held the original. He still owned the property in Rata Avenue.

Yes, it would be time consuming and expensive to have to take it to court but he would win. He would still get exactly what he'd come to Christchurch for.

But it did make a difference, didn't it? Pouring another shot of whisky into the cheap tumbler, Nic paced the soulless motel room.

The satisfaction of achieving exactly what he'd set out to achieve would always be tainted by the dispute. The planned gallery to pay homage to Rata House would be nothing more than a victory crow—an insult to Zanna.

The knock-on effects on his career were enough to anger him all on their own. He was going to have to delay meetings on projects that were starting to line up. A boutique lakeside hotel in Geneva. A warehouse redevelopment on the banks of the Thames in London. The ambitious resort planned for the stretch of beach on the Hibiscus Coast north of Auckland in New Zealand that had been the reason he'd come here for the talks with Prime Property two weeks ago.

Well…that wasn't going to happen now. He had no intention of working with the Scallions again. A short phone call to Donald was all it took to let him know that he couldn't continue to work with a company that resorted to underhanded and illegal tactics like poisoning protected trees. He left Donald in no doubt about how stupid his son had been to come here and try and put the boot in and gloat over the fact that Zanna's property had finally changed hands.

He didn't add that he would never forgive the fact that Blake had unwittingly managed to destroy the connection he'd found with Zanna because it was none of their business. But by the time he ended the call Nic knew he had identified the real core of his anger.

He couldn't win in the end on this one because he'd lost something that had nothing to do with business. Something huge. Yes, the land was the only real connection he still had with his parents and that almost forgotten life but, if that was all he had, there would only ever be memories of how special it had been. Fragments of emotion that would be fleeting echoes of how it had felt to have a home. To belong.

Pour aimer et être aimé.

To love and be loved.

When he was with Zanna, the feeling wasn't a memory. It was real. More than real because it held the magic of a promise that it could always be there. That place was irrelevant because that feeling of home and safety was to do with who Zanna was, not where she lived.

He didn't need a handful of cards spread out beneath a flickering candelabra to read his future if he lost what he'd found so recently. It might be full to the brim with professional satisfaction, public accolades and more money than he could ever spend, but on one level it would be meaningless.

That level had been safely locked away for as long as he could remember but it had been released now and it was too big and too shapeless to ever catch and restrain again.

He loved Zanna. It was as simple as that.

And hadn't she all but said that she'd fallen in love with him?

Do you often have to sleep with potential sellers, Nic? Get them to fall in love with you so that they'll be only too happy to fall into line?

With a groan, Nic reached for the bottle again and unscrewed the metal cap. Poised to pour another shot, he paused. His gaze shifted to the Formica bench of the kitchenette with its electric jug and sachets of probably dreadful coffee.

He let go of the bottle.

Strong coffee was what he needed now. And a bit more time before it was safe to hit the road again.

To go back to where he belonged.

With Zanna.

The house was no emptier than it had been ever since Maggie had set off for her journey of discovery weeks ago.

But it felt different.

Zanna could feel the cavern of that emptiness below her from the eyrie of her studio in the turret.

The spirit of joy the house had always contained was gone, destroyed by a tidal wave of anger and grief.

It was just a house in the end, wasn't it? Without the people, it was haunted by ghosts. Maggie's. Nic's. The ghost of the frightened child she had been when she'd come here and the broken person she'd been when she'd returned from London last year. Maybe the most unbearable ghost right now was the person she was when she was with Nic. The person she had wanted to be for the rest of her life.

She still needed to keep moving because, if she didn't, these emotions would suffocate her. Her hands moved of their own accord to select brushes and paints. The only available canvas was large but that was fine. She had something huge inside that needed to come out. She couldn't have consciously chosen a subject if she'd tried so she didn't spare a thought for a preliminary sketch or even a mental image of where she was headed. This was just an exercise to release some of her anguish. To channel it into a symbol of some kind, perhaps, so that she could then choose to either remove it from her life entirely or keep it as a reminder to make her future choices with more care.

The subject chose itself and it wasn't really a surprise to discover that it was going to be a portrait of Dominic Brabant. What was surprising was how well imprinted he was on her soul for the perfect shape of his face and hands and body to be emerging with such ease and precision. Cruel of her subconscious to pick the scene it had but she knew better than to mess with what was happening inside her head and her heart by trying to change what needed to be expressed.

And besides…this could quite possibly be the best painting she had ever done. As the minutes ticked into hours Zanna was aware of an excitement stealing into the turbulent mix of her emotions. It was a rare thing to find that her mind and hands and spirit were in synch enough to be producing something that felt so right from a creative point of view.

She had caught the moment perfectly and she had to blink away tears as she added the final touches to the work. The twilight of a late summer's evening. The flickering light of small logs burning in the chiminea and echoed by the candelabra on the small table. The posture and intensity of the man holding the guitar. She could almost feel the softness of the tousled waves of his hair. Hear the notes of those words of love in the most beautiful language of the world.

Feel the way those hands had touched and held her soul.

It hadn't all been an act, had it? An expert lover could have learned how to inflame a woman's desire by unbraiding her hair and touching her face as though his fingers wanted to know her features as intimately as his eyes did, but could passion be combined with such… tenderness if it was simply playing a role?

No. She didn't believe she had imagined that he felt as strongly as she did. She had felt the truth in that moment of silence when he'd admitted that he felt as emotionally unbalanced as she did.

But could she trust what she believed?

Given her track record, probably not.

Given how exhausted she was, having channelled an excess of energy into her painting, this wasn't the time to even try and decide what she could trust.

She had to sleep but the thought of going down to her own bed and sleeping alone only brought another wave of misery. Better to stay here and curl up on the antique chaise longue that had been donated to her studio when it had become too ratty to grace the formal living room downstairs. It would be softer than the floor and she was tired enough to consider that a viable option.

Zanna didn't need to leave the lights on to have the image she'd just painted as her last thought before she slipped into an exhausted slumber.

Without needing the adrenaline rush of speed to burn off anger, it took a lot longer to get back to the city.

Propping the bike on its stand, Nic pulled off his helmet and hung it over the handlebars, before turning to look at the silent silhouette of Rata House. It was completely dark from where he was standing. Hardly surprising when he checked his watch to find it was after three a.m.

Zanna would be sound asleep.

Would she be frightened by a knock on the door? He didn't want to frighten her.

Would she guess that he had come back because he couldn't stay away?

But she didn't know he loved her, did she? Would she even believe him when he told her?

Of course she'd been upset. He'd known how fragile that trust was—how it wouldn't survive an additional blow.

He'd hurt her and it was unbearable.

His feet took him, unbidden, through the wrought-iron gate and up the mossy, brick pathway. The stalk of a rough leaf, propelled by a stiff breeze, hit his cheek hard enough to sting and he could almost smell the decay of the dying trees as he veered towards the veranda of the main part of the house.

He peered through the stained-glass panels on either side of the front door, hoping to see a glimmer of light from the end of the hallway that led to the kitchen, but he could see nothing. He could still smell something, though. The musty, decayed smell of the trees seemed to be getting stronger and it was oddly pungent, as though some of those mysterious herbs in Zanna's shop were being burnt.

Sure enough, a glance towards the door of the shop entrance showed a flicker of light. The kind of light that candles would produce and Zanna was very fond of candles, wasn't she? He could remember how many of them had been burning on the counter that day he'd gone in to see her. And the way she'd held her hair back, out of danger, as she'd leaned in to blow them out.

Was she in the shop? Unpacking some of the stock, perhaps, because she believed the deal was off and she needed to reopen her business? He retraced his steps and went to knock on the shop door.

'It's only me,' he called, as he knocked. 'Nic. I need to talk to you, Zanna.'

The only response was the tapping of the 'Closed' sign on the glass of the door as it reverberated to his knock. There were stained-glass panels here, too and the candlelight was much stronger.

So was the smell.

The tendrils of smoke coming from the gap beneath the door were unmistakeable evidence that something was terribly wrong.

Spellbound was on fire.

'*Zanna…*' Nic pounded on the door with a clenched fist. He wrenched at the handle but the door was firmly locked.

Was she even inside the shop?

Down the steps again and Nic stared up at the house. Her bedroom was directly above the shop and below the turret room that contained her studio. Smoke rose and he'd heard somewhere that more people died of smoke inhalation than got burned to death in a fire.

Where was she?

The sound of a sharp crack and then a fizzing noise as though some flammable material had exploded came from within the shop and suddenly he could see the shape of flames through the coloured panels. The smoke gushed out and curled away into the night air.

Running, Nic made his way back to the house door.

He pulled out his phone and punched in the three digit emergency number.

'*Fire*,' he yelled. 'Number thirty-two, Rata Avenue. *Hurry*—there's someone inside the house.'

For a few seconds Nic made a panicked search for some kind of weapon he could use to break a window and get access to the house. A branch from one of the rata trees? The trees were virtually dead so it would be easy to break off a thick piece of wood.

Dying trees…water…the galvanised bucket. The connection took only a microsecond and it felt like Nic had the spare house key in his hand almost by the time he'd completed the thought process. Muscles in his jaw were bunched so tightly he could feel his teeth aching as he finally turned the key and shoved the door open.

The hallway was black. Even if he'd been able to locate a light switch it wouldn't have helped much but enough light was coming from behind to illuminate the thick smoke that was already obscuring half the sweep of the staircase. So much light Nic's head swivelled. Had the emergency services arrived without the use of any sirens?

No. To his horror, he saw that one of the glass panes in the bay window of the shop had blown out. It looked as though flames were hurling themselves into the night air, seeking fuel like some kind of famished, wild animal. The dry leaves and branches of one of the rata trees were close enough to provide exactly what was being sought. Spurts of flame were shooting upwards into the tree and expanding like a mushroom cloud. Illuminating the witch's hat of the turret and the dark windows beneath it.

Any thought of how dangerous it would be to go inside the house simply didn't occur to Nic. In that moment it wouldn't have mattered how quickly he might be overcome by smoke or whatever horrible fumes it might contain.

Zanna was in the house and nothing else mattered.

Nic bunched up the soft fabric of his T-shirt to try and make some protection to cover his mouth and nose. He ran into the smoke and took the stairs two at a time. The heat around him increased but there were no visible flames in here. Holding onto the carved newel post at the top of the stairs, he took a moment to orient himself.

Maggie's room. The bathroom. A spare bedroom. Zanna's room was two doors down on the right just before the spiral stairs that led to the turret. Directly over the shop and where the inferno was gathering pace. He pushed himself on. He had to take a breath and even through the bunched fabric he could taste the smoke and feel the heat and the inadequate level of oxygen the air contained.

But he was in her bedroom.

'Zanna? *Zanna…*' The effort to shout required another breath, which made him cough and draw more smoke into his lungs.

The bedroom was empty.

Smoke had now reached as far as the narrow spiral staircase and it felt thicker here than it had anywhere else. Of course it did. Smoke rose and this was the very top of the old house, in a direct vertical line from where the fire had started.

The door at the top of the stairs was closed. He had to feel for the handle. He turned it and pushed.

No…

The door was locked?

Why?

Nic banged on the wood. 'Zanna. *Zanna*… Are you in there?' She had to be in there because the door was bolted from the inside. 'There's a *fire*…'

He could hear the approaching wail of sirens now. He could hear the sound of glass breaking and then people shouting. What he couldn't hear was any sound from within the round room in the turret.

Zanna's room. Her refuge. This was where she would have gone when she couldn't bear to be in the same room as him, he just knew it.

Was she already unconscious from breathing in too much smoke?

Bracing himself, Nic gathered all the strength he could muster and slammed his shoulder against the door.

And then he did it again.

Zanna had never been so deeply asleep. So deeply drawn into the dream that had begun with the last image she'd seen before slipping into unconsciousness. She was in her courtyard garden, surrounded by the sound of the song Nic was singing as he plucked the strings of that old guitar. She was dancing by the light of the candelabra, wearing something soft and floaty—the soft velvet robe she'd been wearing the day Nic had first walked into Spellbound?

She could smell the aroma of the wood burning in the chiminea. Could feel its heat. She could even hear the words of the song Nic was singing. She knew they were in French but she could understand them so easily.

Ne me quitte pas…don't leave me…

She could hear her own name in the chorus. That was new…

Zanna...*Zanna...*

The dancing in her dream had to stop. The ground was shaking. As Zanna's mind was reluctantly dragged back into consciousness she pushed her eyelids open. Where was she?

She could make out the bare wooden floorboards that looked familiar enough but everything else was so hazy. She was surrounded by her paintings but they seemed obscured by a thick fog. The smell of the fog was weird and Zanna realised how short of breath she was. It was an effort to fill her lungs and when she tried, it was uncomfortable enough to make her cough. And that sucked more of the fog in and made her cough again even more harshly.

Nic heard the cough. The mix of relief that Zanna was in the room and fear that she might already be too overcome by the smoke somehow gave him the strength to summon a last burst of reserves. With this final punishing blow, the wood splintered around the doorhandle and Nic fell into the room, along with an enveloping cloud of thick, hot smoke.

He was on his knees but he could see the shape of Zanna, hunched on the floor beside the old couch. Pushing up with his arm sent a vicious shaft of pain through the shoulder he'd used to batter down the door. It hadn't been possible to keep his face covered while he'd been trying to break through the door and he'd inhaled enough smoke to make his lungs burn painfully as well. The coughing was constant now and a wave of dizziness assaulted him as he crawled towards Zanna to pull her into his arms.

'Fire...' He choked the word out. *'Have to...get... you out.'*

Zanna was stumbling, racking coughs making her double over. Nic kept a grip on her arms that went beyond firmness. A part of his brain registered the fact that he could be causing her pain but it couldn't be helped. Somehow, he had to get them downstairs and there was no way he could carry her down that narrow spiral staircase. Not with only one arm that was obeying commands.

There was a fire escape outside her bedroom window. A wrought-iron ladder that was attached to the weatherboards and ran down to the roof of the veranda. Or would that be unusable now? Had the flames from the burning tree crossed the gap and joined with whatever horror was rising from the shop below?

The passage down the spiral stairs was a barely controlled fall but he caught Zanna with his uninjured arm at the bottom and cushioned her impact. With one arm around her waist he crawled forward, dragging her with him. It was too difficult to breathe and Zanna seemed barely conscious. He couldn't remember what direction they needed to go in. He just knew they had to keep moving.

To stay still would mean certain death for both of them.

Zanna was only dimly aware of what was happening. She knew she was in Nic's arms. She could feel the soft smoothness of that leather jacket and the strength of his muscles as he tried to carry her. But she could feel that strength ebbing as well. The dizziness was overwhelming and her eyes were stinging so much it was impossible to open them. Fear was there, too. She knew something terrible was happening.

But she was in Nic's arms so how bad could it be? She just had to try and help him. Had to stay close.

Then she felt the grip of those arms loosen and the smoothness of that soft leather slip away. There was new pressure now. Stronger. Heavily gloved hands that were pulling her upwards. Roughly clad arms that were holding her. Alien faces obscured by masks, making sounds that resembled speech but were totally incomprehensible.

There was movement, too. Rapid and purposeful. The temperature changed and became cold. More hands were pulling at Zanna, tangling themselves in her hair painfully. Something was on her face, covering her mouth and nose. She tried to push it away because she needed to breathe. *Had* to breathe. She was suffocating.

'Leave it on.' The voice was suddenly clear. 'It's oxygen, love. You need it. You've inhaled a lot of smoke.'

Zanna tried to open her eyes. She tried to say something but the effort only provoked a new fit of coughing. She could hear someone else coughing nearby. There were sounds of people shouting and heavy activity. Generators or engines humming. Water gushing and hitting solid objects under pressure. Someone talking more quietly, right beside her.

'Just concentrate on your breathing, Zanna. I'm putting a clip on your finger so we can see what the oxygen level in your blood is doing. Then I'm going to listen to your chest. Are you hurting anywhere?'

She shook her head. How did they know her name? Who were these people? She made a new effort to open her eyes and caught a glimpse of uniformed people surrounding her. One was holding a stethoscope. Another was wrapping a cuff around her arm. She was on a stretcher and there was another one within touching distance if she reached out.

Nic was sitting on that stretcher.

Oh…thank God…Nic was here. Those patchy memories of being held so tightly in his arms hadn't been a dream. She had sent him away but he was here again.

He'd come back. The way he had that first time when she'd been so sure she wouldn't see him again.

Why had he come back this time?

To apologise, perhaps? To say goodbye?

How hard would that be?

She didn't want him to stay. She couldn't trust him. But it would have been better to have never had to see him again.

But hadn't he just saved her from something terrible? How could you not trust someone who had saved your life?

Confusion exacerbated the dizziness that was already clouding her brain.

Nic's face was blackened. He was holding a mask to his mouth and nose and coughing wretchedly. Someone was touching his arm and he gave an anguished yell of pain that Zanna was sure she could feel herself.

'Looks like it's dislocated, mate. Hang on and we'll get you some pain relief before we do anything else.'

The paramedic was blocking her view of Nic now but knowing he'd been hurt made her chest tighten and it was even harder to try and breathe.

Through the narrow windows above his head Zanna could see flashing lights. In the split second before the dizziness took hold again and forced her eyes shut, she looked out of the back doors of what she realised was an ambulance.

She could see the fire engines parked close by. A crowd of heavily uniformed figures were bustling about, dealing with equipment and hoses. And she could see the charred branches of the trees, devoid of any leaves now, and she could even see the black holes that had been the windows of Spellbound—missing teeth in a broken face.

Her house had been burned. Her home was gone.

The tears felt like overheated oil as they seared Zanna's eyes. She held them tightly shut. This was way too much to cope with.

'The cats.' Her words came out as a harsh croak and she didn't even recognise them herself. She caught the arm of the paramedic who was taking her blood pressure. The movement was agitated enough to make him abandon the task and lift the mask from her face.

'You'll have to say that again, love. I couldn't hear you properly.'

'Cats...'

'Sorry?'

'Cats.' Nic's voice came from behind the paramedic. 'There are three cats. Black.' He coughed and Zanna could hear the rasp as he sucked in a new breath. 'They would have been inside the house. You have to find them.'

'I'll pass it on. Nobody's allowed in the house yet. They're still trying to make sure the fire's contained.' The mask was fitted back to Zanna's face. 'Try not to worry. Someone will find your cats.'

She let her eyes drift shut again.

Nic was here but she didn't know why.

Her beloved house was destroyed.

Maggie was on the other side of the world.

And the M&Ms were missing. Dead?

Her brain hurt from trying to take it all in. Her lungs hurt from trying to breathe. But most of all her heart was hurting.

And it was unbearable.

CHAPTER ELEVEN

HE HADN'T FELT like this since his mother had died and they'd come to take him away.

So alone, with an unknown future that was huge and empty and forbidding.

Except this time *was* different.

He really had been alone then and he'd learned to rely only on himself. Not to let anyone close enough to make it a problem if they disappeared.

But then he'd met Zanna. How had she got so close, so fast? As if there'd been a Zanna-shaped hole in his soul that she had just slipped into?

He could have lost her last night and the enormity of facing that made everything else meaningless in comparison.

Was this love? This feeling that he could never be the best person he was capable of being without her? That an unknown future could be bright and enticing instead of something that had to be faced with grim fortitude?

Nic had the curious feeling of coming full circle. Of finding what he'd resisted searching for all his life, only to discover it had been back where he'd started. Physically and emotionally. In the only place he'd known a family. With the only person he'd ever fallen in love with.

He had to tell Zanna.

They'd been separated as soon as they'd arrived at the hospital. The first attempt to relocate his shoulder had been unsuccessful and then there'd been X-rays and drugs that had taken a long time to sleep off.

With his arm in a sling he'd finally been able to trace where Zanna was in the hospital, only to be told that she was currently asleep and not to be disturbed. When he went back again, she was awake but talking to a police detective who was investigating the fire.

'Come back in a couple of hours,' the nursing staff advised. 'Miss Zelensky's not going anywhere just yet. She needs a good rest.'

She was still asleep when Nic returned yet again but this time he wasn't going anywhere. He sat on a chair near her bed and listened to the faint rasp of her breathing.

And waited.

Sleep was the best escape.

There had been visits from doctors. A portable X-ray machine had been brought in to take images of her lungs and a respiratory technician had taken a long time to test their function. The interview with the police detective had been tiring and upsetting because nobody could tell her whether the cats were okay. It had been such a relief to drift back into unconsciousness.

Being awake meant too many things clamouring for attention. Practical things like whether she still had any clothes available and if there was enough money in the bank to cover temporary accommodation. Physical things like how long it would be before it felt easy to breathe again and how soon she would have enough of a voice to call Maggie so that she could tell her about what had happened now. The emotional things were the worst, though. That horrible feeling of knowing that something disastrous had happened and the future had changed for ever. A bit like that emotional tornado she'd found herself in after finding Simon in bed with Brie. A lot like the terrifying abyss of knowing she would never see her parents again.

She'd had Maggie then but now she had nobody. Not here, anyway. Not close enough to hold her and make her believe that it would all be all right in the end. She had a blurry memory of Nic being in the ambulance with her but she hadn't seen him since.

He'd risked his life to save her. The police detective had told her that and the nursing staff obviously thought he was a hero.

'He did come,' someone told her. 'But you were asleep. He'll be back.'

To say goodbye?

Maybe she didn't want him to come back.

She saw him the moment she opened her eyes. Sitting in the chair, slumped forward a little with his elbows on his knees and his hands shading his eyes, as if he was trying to find a solution to the problems of the world.

For a moment she just gazed at him, remembering the first time she'd seen him. When he'd walked into her shop and she'd felt the blast of testosterone and the thrill of thinking he wanted *her*.

Amazing that someone could still exude that kind of masculine power from such a relaxed position. Could still seem commanding when his clothes were streaked with grime and there was a big tear in his jeans. Could still be so incredibly sexy with a couple of days of stubble and lines of weariness etched deeply into his face.

Nobody would ever guess the vulnerable part of him that was so well hidden but, for Zanna, that knowledge would always be there. He needed her love but already she could feel it being locked away. A part of the past. Was that for the best? He might not have wanted it anyway.

Her inward breath caught and made her cough and Nic's hands dropped as he lifted his head.

For a long, long moment they simply held each other's gaze.

'Hey…' Nic's voice was quiet. A bit croaky. 'You're awake. How are you feeling?'

'Oh—okay, I think.' Her voice was still hoarse. She pushed herself more upright in the bed. 'Are you?' He had his arm in a sling.

The single nod was familiar now. 'I dislocated my shoulder. It's been put back. I just need to be careful with it for a bit.'

'No bike-riding, then.' Zanna tried to smile but it wasn't going to happen.

'No.'

A silence fell that she didn't want to continue because that could be the moment that Nic told her he was leaving. That he was giving up on his music-school project or whatever it was he'd come for because it had become all too messy and that he was going back to London. Or France. Somewhere as far away from her as he could get.

Some things had to be said, however.

'I hear you saved my life,' she managed. 'Thank you.'

'I just happened to be in the right place at the right time. It wasn't a matter of choice.'

'There's always a choice. You didn't have to put your own life at risk.'

But Nic shook his head. His look suggested she was missing the point.

'Have the police talked to you yet?'

'No. I saw an officer at the house. He was making sure nothing got looted but he let me in when I told him why I was there. I've got your bag and wallet and things. And some clothes for you. They might smell a bit smoky but they're okay.'

'You've been to the house?'

'Yes. I needed to do something while you were asleep.'

'Did you find the cats?'

'No. Sorry. I've left some food out in the courtyard for when they come back.'

'How...how bad is it?'

'I couldn't get into the shop. That's where the worst of the damage is and there was a fire investigation crew in there. As far as I can see, it's only smoke and water damage in the rest of the house but...it's not pretty, Zanna. I've called Pete. He's going to come over and see whether it makes a difference to whether it can still be moved but he can't come for a few days.'

But Zanna didn't seem to be interested in whether the project would have to be abandoned. Like she hadn't realised how stupid it had been to suggest he'd had a choice about whether or not he'd go into a burning house.

She'd been inside. Of course he'd had no choice.

'They're saying the fire was deliberately lit.'

'What?'

'There's apparently clear evidence that an accelerant was used. In the shop.' Zanna coughed again and reached for the glass of water on the bedside locker.

'I've told the police all about Blake being there. About all the trouble there's been.'

Had she told them about him as well? About the apparent deception that had led to her agreeing to sell the house?

It didn't matter. Nic's opinion of himself probably wasn't any worse than what the police would think.

'This is my fault.' He pressed his fingers to his forehead before pushing them through his hair. 'I called Don. I told him that I wouldn't be working with him again. I knew they'd be angry. I suspect the company will be in big financial strife if the new resort project gets canned. And he knew I'd bought your place. They would have made a lot of money out of that if they'd ever got hold of it.' He had to get to his feet. 'But to do *that* as some kind of revenge... You could have died, Zanna.'

'It's not all your fault, Nic.'

'What's not all his fault?'

Two police officers were standing in the door of the room. Zanna recognised one of them as the detective she'd spoken to earlier.

'Did you find him?' she demanded. 'Have you arrested Blake Scallion?'

'We've talked to him, yes.'

'And?' Nic was scowling.

'He denies any involvement. He's telling a rather different story, in fact.' The detective turned to Nic. 'You're Dominic Brabant, I assume?'

The single nod answered the query.

'And you've recently purchased thirty-two Rata Avenue from Miss Zelensky?'

'Yes.'

'And you own the adjoining property?'

'That's correct.'

'I understand you're into property development. That you've worked with the Scallions over the last few years off and on.'

'Not any more. Not after what I've learned about how they've treated Zanna and her aunt. They—'

'What did you intend to do with the house? It would be in the way of any development, wouldn't it?'

'Are you suggesting *I* set the fire?' Nic's tone was dangerous. 'When Zanna was inside?'

'And you were conveniently there to rescue her?' The detective's expression said it seemed plausible.

'That's ridiculous.' The fierceness of her words made Zanna cough again. 'We're…we're…'

What were they, exactly? Or what had they been? Friends? Lovers? Soul-mates? She didn't know what they had been and it made her feel helpless. Knowing that whatever it was wasn't there any more made it all seem irrelevant anyway. She shifted her gaze to Nic as if that could help her make some kind of sense of what had happened between them but he was glaring at the detective who was speaking again.

'The suggestion came from Mr Scallion but it's not an unreasonable scenario. I imagine the house is insured. It would be more profitable to make a claim than pay demolition costs. And hasn't a fair percentage of the contents already been put into storage?'

'Blake's lying,' Zanna said fiercely. 'He's been threatening us for years. He poisoned our trees.' She made a frustrated sound. 'You don't know what you're talking about. The house is going to be shifted, not demolished. We've bought land…'

Except that contract hadn't been signed yet, had it?

The papers had all been drawn up but the owners were overseas until next week so couldn't add their signatures.

'And of course Nic was around,' Zanna added. 'He's been staying with me since...'

Was it only last week? Would they ask how long she'd known him before she'd let him stay?

This was all crazy and she seemed to be making it worse. Zanna pressed her lips together and shut her eyes. She needed to think.

'We'd like you to come down to the station, Mr Brabant. We need to ask you some more questions and take a statement.'

'Fine. The sooner we get this sorted the better. I'd like a solicitor present as well.'

Zanna's eyes snapped open. Were they *arresting* Nic? What evidence did they have, other than circumstantial? Not for one moment had she thought he'd had anything to do with the fire but—just for a heartbeat—she could feel the roller-coaster of the doubts and perceived betrayal she had been riding for the last few days.

Was there something in what the police were suggesting?

Something she just didn't want to see because part of her still wanted to believe in Nic?

She'd ripped up the contract and potentially made it impossible for him to achieve his dream. He would have been angry about that, wouldn't he?

He'd worked with Blake before. Was it so impossible to imagine he would do it again?

But why would he have risked his own life to save her from a fire he'd started himself?

Or had he misjudged the timing of events?

Nic chose that moment to turn and look at her. He

seemed about to say something but then he met her eyes and his mouth closed.

He turned again, without saying a word, and accompanied the police officers out of the room.

Zanna was pushing her bed covers back as a nurse came into the room moments later.

'What do you need, love?'

'I need to go home,' Zanna said, her voice breaking. 'Now. Could you help me find my clothes, please?'

CHAPTER TWELVE

THE TREES WERE BARE.

Whatever leaves had still clung to their branches had either been burned away or just given up the battle and fallen to the ground. The trunk of the tree closest to the shop was blackened and the smaller branches were gone, their stumps poking into a grey sky that threatened rain at any moment. The house looked naked without the leafy screen. Exposed to the eyes of curious onlookers who stood behind the bright orange 'Police Emergency' tape that circled the front of the house and peered at the evidence of trauma with morbid fascination.

One of those figures was familiar. It was only days ago that she'd seen her solicitor, Keith Watson, and that meeting had been a celebration of a secured future for Rata House. A future that looked as if it had been snatched away.

'Suzanna.' Keith came towards her as the taxi pulled away. 'I couldn't believe it when I heard about the fire. Are you all right?'

No. Zanna was a very long way from being all right. Force of habit made her stand a little straighter, though.

'I was lucky,' she told Keith. 'I got rescued. It could have been a lot worse.'

'Indeed it could. How on earth did the fire start?'

'Apparently it was arson.'

Keith looked shocked. And then he looked around them as though worried that someone might have overheard. 'Are you allowed inside?' He gestured towards the police officer who stood on the path on the other side of the tape.

'It's my house. Why wouldn't I be allowed inside? I need to see how bad it is.'

Keith lowered his voice. 'If they know it was arson, then it's a crime scene. Let me have a word with the officer.'

Zanna waited on the edge of the crowd, thankful for the hood of her sweatshirt giving her a perceived privacy. This was hard, not being alone when she had to cope with the shock of seeing her home like this. She wasn't even sure she wanted to go inside yet.

Steeling herself, she looked past the ruined trees. The glass panes of the bay window of Spellbound were broken and had been roughly boarded over. The weatherboards of the house were blackened and larger pieces of debris from the shop had been piled in a charred heap at the bottom of the steps.

Despite herself, she was drawn closer. She needed to see the worst of it.

She was closer to the rest of the onlookers now. Beside a trio of high-school students.

'Oh, my God,' a blonde girl said. 'I can't believe this.'

'It's awful,' her companion agreed. 'Where are we going to go after school now, Jen?'

Zanna's head turned. Holding Jen's hand was a lanky youth with a flop of hair that covered one eye.

'I told you about this shop, Stevie, didn't I? It was so cool.'

'Bit of a mess now. Let's go and get a burger or something.'

'It must have been one of those candles.' Jen still sounded fascinated by the drama. 'On the counter, remember? Maybe one of them didn't get put out. It's really sad, isn't it?' She leaned closer to the boy, who obligingly put his arm around her shoulders as they turned to leave.

Zanna had to blink back tears. Maybe the jellybean spell had worked but there wouldn't be a stream of teenage girls coming into Spellbound as word of mouth spread.

There wouldn't be anyone coming in for herbal tea and organic cake either. Spellbound, as it had been, didn't exist any more.

Keith was waving at her. Holding the plastic tape up with his other hand. 'We can go in and get any necessities you might need but we can't stay long. And you can have a look but we're not to go beyond the tape or touch anything in the shop. They haven't finished the investigation yet.'

Zanna nodded. She was thankful that Keith was here. A kindly, middle-aged man who had known both her and Maggie for years. He would look after her if she couldn't cope and right now she wasn't at all sure how well she was going to cope.

They started with the shop, skirting the pile of debris and climbing the steps to look over the tape past the half-open door.

Water still dripped from intact but charred beams in the ceiling of the room. The smell of the fire was still overpowering. The dead, unpleasant odour of charred wood, wet ashes and a peculiar mixture of pungent oils and herbs. A blackened, stinking layer of rubbish covered the floor and what was left of the counter.

Zanna shut her eyes. Had she shut the door properly last night or had she been distracted by that horrible sensation of being watched and then forgotten completely when she'd gone in to confront Nic with what she'd been told? What if the cats had gone back to their favourite new sleeping place on that pile of clothing?

She choked back a sob and Keith put his arm around her shoulders.

'Let's go into the main part of the house. It can't be as bad as where the fire started.'

It wasn't as bad. Or maybe Zanna was being protected by the numbness she could feel enveloping her brain and her heart. Fatigue washed into every cell in her body and it was an effort to make her legs move to follow Keith. She just needed to get this over with and then she could find somewhere to curl up and go to sleep again for a while.

Everything looked black and dirty and smelt horrible. How could smoke do so much damage in such a short space of time? It was like someone had taken a colour image of everything and then made a very bad job of trying to turn it into an arty sepia print. The colours were all wrong on the flowers on her bedroom wall and when she touched one, all she did was make a blackened smear that obliterated the lines of the petals.

It was heartbreaking.

'Do you want to look upstairs? In the turret?'

Zanna shook her head. The last thing she remembered clearly from last night was finishing that painting—an image torn from her soul. She couldn't bear to see that ruined.

'I don't need to see any more,' she said quietly. 'I just want to check to see whether the cats have been back for any food and then I'll have to find somewhere to stay.'

'We'll organise a motel. Or you could come home with me. Janice would love to be able to look after you.'

It was a kind offer. She should feel grateful but the numbness was blunting any kind of response and Zanna was actually grateful for that. If she couldn't feel small things, maybe she'd stop feeling the huge, overwhelming things as well.

'Have you contacted your insurance company?'

'No.'

'It might be best if I do that for you. It's going to complicate things a bit that the property's been sold so recently. And that the fire was deliberate. It could get messy.'

Zanna simply nodded. She couldn't face any of the bureaucracy that this situation would create. She didn't have the energy and what was the point? Everything was ruined.

The food that Nic had left in the courtyard for the cats hadn't been touched. As if that was the last straw, Zanna sank into one of the wrought-iron chairs and closed her eyes, gathering that comforting numbness around her like a cloak.

'Have you been in touch with Maggie? Does she know about this?'

Zanna shook her head again.

'Would you like me to do that for you?'

'No. But I haven't got my phone. I don't imagine the landline will be working?'

'I wouldn't think so. They will have turned off the

services to the house after the fire. I'll have Maggie's number in my phone. Would you like to use that?'

Zanna wanted to shake her head again. She didn't want to have to tell Maggie about this. Didn't want to have anything pierce the anaesthetic cloak that was working so well to numb her emotional pain. It would be the middle of the night over there and Maggie would answer her phone already knowing that something was very wrong.

'She'll need to know,' Keith said gently. 'And I'm sure she'd want to know as soon as possible. This has been her home for a very long time and we both know how much she loves it.'

So Zanna nodded instead of shaking her head and let Keith find the number and call it. Then he handed her the phone and walked back into the kitchen to give her some privacy.

It rang and rang and went to voicemail. Hearing Maggie's voice was enough to stab a huge hole in the numbness and suddenly all Zanna wanted was to hear the voice for real and not on a recorded message so she ended the call and immediately pushed redial.

This time it was answered but then there was only silence.

'Hello? Maggie—are you there?'

She could hear something. Someone speaking faintly in a language she didn't recognise. Russian? No…it must be Romanian. Had Maggie lost her phone?

'Hello?' The query was more tentative now. 'Can someone hear me?'

'Ah…' A rich male voice was clear. 'At last. It's hard to work a different phone. Is that Suzanna?'

'Yes...' The English was perfect but heavily accented. 'Is that...Dimitry?'

'Yes. I am so pleased you called. I have been trying to find your number but couldn't access the contacts menu.'

The numbness was evaporating painfully fast, as if it was being peeled away from Zanna's skin.

'Where's Maggie, Dimitry? What's happened?'

'Maggie is in a hospital in Bucharest. I brought her here earlier in the night because I was so afraid for her and it seems that she may have had a heart attack. She is having a procedure at the moment but she gave me her phone before they took her away. She asked me to call you.'

'Oh, my God... *No...*'

Keith must have heard her agonised cry because he came out of the house swiftly. With one look at Zanna's face he took the phone from her shaking hand.

'Hello? My name's Keith Watson. I'm with Suzanna. Please tell me what's going on.'

'I do apologise for the length of time this has taken, Mr Brabant. But you understand we had several lines of enquiry to follow up.'

'So I can go now?'

'You won't be needed again until Mr Scallion's trial begins. That probably won't be for a month or so.'

'Did you get hold of Zanna? Does she know about the CCTV footage from the petrol station on Rata Avenue that shows Blake buying the can of petrol?'

'We've been unable to contact her. She left the hospital some hours ago, shortly after we brought you in for the interview. She visited the house but left in a hurry about an hour later, according to the officer we have on the scene. Her mobile phone isn't being answered. It's either switched off or dead or out of range.'

Nic could only nod. His shoulder ached abominably and it felt like days since he had slept. They'd offered him food while he'd been here at the central police station but he hadn't been hungry. The physical discomfort he was in was pale in comparison to the utter weariness of spirit weighing him down.

He would never be able to forget the way Zanna had looked at him from her hospital bed.

As if she thought he could have been responsible for the fire that had almost killed her.

He was too exhausted to feel hurt any more. Or angry, which had been the best way to deal with the hurt. Now he just felt empty.

And a bit lost.

There was only one place in this city that he felt remotely connected with and it wasn't a long walk from the city's biggest police station so it was no real surprise that he automatically headed in the direction of Rata Avenue. He would have to do something about sorting the bike still parked on the street, anyway, given that he wouldn't be riding it back to the hire firm himself.

It was late afternoon now, and beginning to rain, which made the scene of the fire all the more bleak when he arrived there. The broken and boarded windows of the shop made the house look derelict. Haunted, even.

A police officer was sheltering from the rain on the veranda.

'The owner's not here but there's a bloke in there who says he's her solicitor if you want to talk to him.'

Nic didn't bother telling him that he, in fact, was the owner. Or was he? The possession date had been yesterday, hadn't it? Did something like this put an immediate injunction on legal proceedings? Keith would know.

He found Keith in the kitchen, finishing a phone call.

'You can start tomorrow. Nine o'clock. I've arranged a cleaning firm to be here at the same time, so the items for storage can be cleaned before you transport them. I'll be here as well. I want to make sure that everything salvageable is removed.'

He turned to Nic as he ended the call. 'You look terrible.'

'Cheers.'

His tone was grim but Keith's face softened. He stepped forward to grip Nic's uninjured shoulder. 'I've known Suzanna Zelensky since she was six years old,' he said quietly. 'A frightened little girl that Maggie was determined to keep safe. You saved her life last night and—on behalf of Maggie—I want to tell you how much that means.' His voice cracked. 'Just in case Maggie never gets the chance to tell you herself.'

He let go of Nic and cleared his throat. 'I'm sorting out getting the house cleared for you.'

'So the property is legally mine?'

'The possession date was four p.m. yesterday so it was well past by the time the fire started. There's a grey area concerning insurance on the house because nothing had been arranged to cover that separately. I'll talk to the insurance company and we'll start working through that tomorrow. I'll have to look into the purchase of the new land as well, but it looks as if that might have to fall through. Suzanna's not going to be here to sign anything.'

'Why not?' A chill ran down Nic's spine. 'Where is she?'

'Right now she's on a flight to Auckland. She's heading for LA and then London, where she can connect to a flight to Romania. It's going to take too long but it was the best we could do and the airlines have done their best to accommodate a family emergency.'

'What emergency?' Was it the mix of pain and exhaustion that was making his brain feel so sluggish?

'Maggie's had a heart attack. We have no idea how bad it was. Or even if she'll still be alive by the time Suzanna gets there.' Keith shook his head. 'As if the poor girl didn't have enough on her plate as it is. She looked a lot worse than you, Nic, but there was no stopping her.'

A smile tugged at the corner of Nic's mouth. 'She has an amazing spirit. Nobody would stop Zanna being with a person she loved who needed her.'

Keith gave him a curious glance that lingered long enough for Nic to wonder what the older man was thinking.

'I've got a few more calls and notes to make. You might want to have a wander around. I imagine you need a bit of time to decide what you need to do next.'

That was true enough. So many things would have to be put on hold. He might own the land but nothing could be started for the music school until the house was gone and that belonged to Zanna. It would be a couple of days before Pete could get here and give his opinion on whether it could still be moved but Nic didn't want to think about what would happen if it was decided that the damage was too great.

And it wasn't, surely?

With more purpose in his movements, Nic followed Keith's suggestion of wandering around. He took in the revolting mess of the room that had housed the shop but damped down the feeling of defeat the smell and sight of the damage evoked and looked more closely. The windows could be replaced and the stock certainly could. The gap in the internal wall that had let so much smoke into the main part of the house could also be repaired but how complicated that would be depended on how much damage there had been to the supporting beams.

He looked up. The solid beams would always be scarred from the charring but they looked strong enough to be structurally sound. If he went to the room above and tested the floor, he might get an even better idea of whether additional strengthening would solve any issues.

His path took him up the main stairway. He could feel his heart thumping against his ribs as he remembered the last time he'd come up here. The overwhelming fear for Zanna's safety that had driven him through the heat and smoke.

The feeling like it was his own life he was trying to save.

Being in her bedroom added a tightness to his throat that reminded him of how hard it had been to breathe. And no wonder. How much smoke had made it in here to blacken the walls like this? How sad would Zanna have felt to have been standing where he was? All that work. The painstaking hours that encapsulated the birth of a passion. The emerging talent that was such a huge part of who she was. The flowers were ruined.

Or were they?

Rubbing one gently with his finger only made the black smudge thicker but when he licked his finger and concentrated on one tiny patch, the delicate blue of a forget-me-not appeared amongst the grime as if a miniature spotlight had been focused on it. He looked around.

This could be fixed. How would Zanna feel if she could walk in here again and see them as they had been? He could imagine how still she would become. The wonder in her face that would morph into joy.

He could add a lump to the tightness in his throat as he turned away. The odds of him seeing that were virtually nil.

There was no real reason to climb the spiral staircase but maybe he needed some closure. To view the door that was responsible for the pain he was in. To see where Zanna might have died if he hadn't been able to break in.

The smoke had been thick enough to be dangerous but not as bad as it had been a floor below. The sketches and paintings weren't obscured by grimy residue. The images of the cats reminded Nic that he needed to have another look for the M&Ms before he left. The image on the easel was a different one from what had been there the last time he'd been in here.

He stepped closer. And then he stepped back again.

Something huge was squeezing the breath right out of him as he stared at the painting. At his own image that could have been a photograph except that it was too rich for that. He could hear the notes of the guitar strings being plucked. The words of the classic song he'd been singing for Zanna.

Ne me quitte pas.

Don't leave me.

How could she have captured him so perfectly without knowing him well enough to see into his soul?

And if she could really do that, there was no chance she could have believed he would ever do anything to put her in danger.

All that was needed was a chance to be together

again—without something traumatic obscuring what needed to be seen.

Of course Zanna needed time with Maggie right now but soon…

Maybe soon, what she would need would be a reason to come back.

How long would she be away?

Too long?

Or not long enough?

CHAPTER THIRTEEN

'LADIES AND GENTLEMEN, please return to your seats. We will shortly be starting our preparations for landing.'

The announcement came while Zanna was trying to freshen up in the cramped confines of the plane's toilet. She had dragged a brush through her hair, washed her face and managed to apply enough make-up to hide the physical evidence of a long and tiring journey. The train trip through Romania had been enough of a trip in itself but the ensuing roundabout connection of flights from Bucharest to Germany to Singapore and finally back to New Zealand had taken over thirty hours.

As she returned to her seat and complied with the preparation for landing instructions by putting her safety belt on and shoving her bag under the seat in front, the pilot's voice came over the engine noise again.

'Going to be a gorgeous day, folks. Light north-westerly breeze, clear skies and an expected maximum temperature of twenty-eight degrees Celsius. A real Indian summer's day.'

Just as well she'd chosen to wear her favourite orange crop top, Zanna decided—one of the few items she had grabbed during that frantic scramble to pack a bag a month ago, when she'd been so afraid she wouldn't arrive in time to see Maggie alive.

So many panicked hours with no way to communicate with anyone until she'd reached Dimitry, who had been there to meet her flight. Not only was Maggie still alive, she was back at home in Dimitry's castle. The heart attack had been minor and the treatment meant that, with a few lifestyle changes, she would probably be healthier than ever. The moment Zanna had walked into her aunt's embrace she had known that that place was exactly where she needed to be. Where she needed to stay until some healing—both physical and emotional—had taken place.

She might not have come home this soon if Keith hadn't made contact to let her know she was required to give evidence at Blake Scallion's trial for arson. The cards had told Maggie that the conclusion to the trouble was coming and she was already satisfied that karma was intact. Keith had told them that Prime Property had gone into liquidation in the last few days. The Scallions were ruined.

It wasn't the only forecast that had come from the treasured set of cards Zanna had brought over for Maggie.

'The Empress? But she's about marriage and birth…'

'Perhaps it's the birth of a creative child, darling. You might be about to start a period of artwork that will provide fulfilment. I miss your paintings so much. Especially the sunflowers under the stairs. And the ivy in the bathroom.'

That had brought tears to Zanna's eyes but she still wasn't ready to talk about it. Those paintings were gone and she missed them too. Especially that last one. She hadn't wanted to talk about Nic either. It was over. Gone, along with her dreams for the house and her studio.

The plane's wheels jarred on the tarmac and the engines howled as it slowed.

The cards had played a cruel trick, putting up the King of Pentacles as a forthcoming influence for Zanna, but she wouldn't allow herself to see it as representing a person.

Because that would always be Nic's card?

He hadn't even called.

And why would he, when he'd been left thinking that she didn't believe in him?

On top of her drama-queen performance of ripping up that contract and telling him to get out?

She'd been so hurt by the idea of him being associated with Prime Property. She'd felt so betrayed. With the benefit of hindsight she could see that it had been a necessary twist of fate that the unexpected availability of the apartment block had been the catalyst for the inspiration of the music school. If he hadn't purchased the neighbouring property first, he would never have had reason to come to a city that would never boast a coastal resort.

Where was he now? Probably on site at the location of a new project or back in London or France, waiting for decisions to be made so that they could all move forward. Of course the sale of the property hadn't been affected by her ripping up what had only been a copy of a legally binding contract.

The plane had stopped now. The snap of seat-belts being released accompanied movement as everyone began to gather their belongings.

The King of Pentacles was probably to do with all

the money that was waiting in an account after the sale had been finalised. A Midas touch, thanks to Keith, who had been taking care of everything that had needed sorting. At first unbearably weary and then feeling too sad, Zanna had let Maggie take over the intermittent conversations about what was happening and simply accepted her reassurance that things would be as they needed to be in the future. Her beloved aunt needed time to recover herself and she deserved to enjoy the happiness she'd found with Dimitry without having it tainted by worry about her niece's disastrous love life.

And it seemed that there was no hurry. Zanna could take a look while she was here for the trial and the really big decisions could wait until after that. Until she was ready.

Finally, she was. It was time to move forward, in more ways than one.

Hearing herself being paged as she emerged from customs led Zanna to an information desk.

'There's a message for you, Miss Zelensky. A Mr Keith Watson has arranged an elite taxi for you. It's the first one on the corporate taxi rank.'

Zanna smiled her thanks. It was a pleasant surprise not to have to arrange her own transport into the city. Had Maggie made the suggestion during one of those quiet conversations with their solicitor?

The walk to the taxi rank was short but there was enough time to look up and marvel at the clarity of the air here compared to the permanent haze of Europe. This was home and quality of light was something she wanted to infuse into her paintings for the rest of her life. Regular visits to the fairy-tale castle in the Transylvanian

Alps would be a must but this was where she wanted to be based.

She would just have to find somewhere to live.

The first car on the rank was a sleek, dark BMW with a discreet elite logo. Zanna opened the back door.

'Is this the taxi ordered by Watkins and Associates? Going to the Park View Hotel?'

The driver nodded into his mirror and muttered something about luggage that she had difficulty hearing. He was wearing a uniform that included a peaked cap and his mirrored sunglasses were all that she could see in the rear-view mirror.

'Don't worry about luggage. This is the only bag I have.' Sliding onto the comfortable leather upholstery, she dropped the overnight bag beside her. She fastened her safety belt as the car pulled smoothly away from the stand and then tilted her head back and closed her eyes. It was only a short ride into the central city but Zanna didn't feel inclined to engage in meaningless small talk. She needed some time to centre herself and prepare for the emotional impact that would come at some stage today when she had to go to Rata Avenue and make a decision about the final fate of her house.

The ten minutes seemed to stretch longer than even bad traffic could account for. And when she opened her eyes it took several seconds for Zanna to register what part of the city she was in. Or rather what part of the city she was *not* in. They were nowhere near the CBD. She was being driven out of town, in fact, with the last pocket of suburbia now behind them.

What was going on? Zanna's tiredness evaporated, the alarm raised by a potentially dangerous situation providing more than enough fuel to burn it off. She sat up straight as the car slowed to turn off the main road.

Maybe she wasn't being abducted. The last time she'd been on this road had been on the back of Nic's bike when he'd brought her out to see the land that would have been the perfect location for Rata House.

Had Keith arranged this, too? She'd assumed that the sale and purchase agreement for the land out here had been shelved, along with all the other plans in the wake of the fire, but maybe there was something that needed discussion. Was Keith meeting her there?

Her guess about the destination was correct, at any rate. The car slowed again at the ornate wooden gates she remembered and then rolled up a driveway newly shingled with small white pebbles. Past the lake with the willow trees and jetty and the little rowboat and there was the old stone stable building, but Zanna barely registered it. She remembered the stretch of grass like a small park and she could remember imagining Rata House in the middle of it.

Her fatigue must be a lot worse than she'd realised for her imagination to be playing a trick like this. For her to be seeing exactly what she had imagined. Her house—only it couldn't be her house because this was a younger version. Freshly painted, with a new slate roof, copper guttering and downpipes and new, wide veranda steps flanked by tubs of brilliant orange, red and yellow nasturtiums.

Even more fantastically, there were tendrils of wisteria already climbing up the wrought-iron of the veranda decoration and borders around the house were filled with the kind of old-fashioned flowers Zanna loved best. Roses and lavender and pansies. A profusion of colour that wrapped the house with a ribbon of joy. Most amazing of all were two large rata trees planted in front.

Completely lost for words, Zanna climbed out of the car very, very slowly after the driver opened the door for her. For a full minute she just stood there, completely stunned.

And then she looked around for someone to tell her what on earth was going on. How this magic had happened. But she was alone with her chauffeur.

'Do you know?' she asked. 'Who did this?'

In response, he shrugged off the uniform jacket to reveal a black T-shirt. Took off the peaked cap he was wearing. Removed the mirrored sunglasses.

And Zanna gasped.

'Nic.'

Oh, dear Lord, he looked exactly as he had in every dream she'd had of him in the last month. The rumpled hair and those gorgeous dark eyes. The shadowing on his jaw and that sexy hint of a slow smile that hadn't surfaced yet.

'What do you think?'

'I...' Zanna's head swerved to check that she hadn't imagined the house and then it swerved back because it was more important that she wasn't imagining that Nic was here. 'But I don't understand... How did you do this? *Why*?'

'I wanted to give you something to come back for.' The words were quiet. 'I wanted to see you again.'

'Oh...*Nic*...' Laughter was warring with tears. 'You could have just asked. If I'd known you wanted to see me I would have gone anywhere.'

She saw understanding dawn in his eyes and the lines of tension dissolve in his face. She saw the beginnings of that smile but then he was too close to see any more and she didn't need to see because she could feel. The strength of his arms around her as he held her so tightly. The softness of his lips as he kissed her and then kissed her again.

And then he took her hand. 'Come and see,' he invited. 'I want to show you everything.'

But Zanna stopped before they'd even reached the veranda steps. 'How?' She demanded. 'How on earth was this even possible?'

'It was a logistical nightmare,' Nic admitted. 'Pete and I have been working pretty much twenty-four seven since we started, which was probably about when you arrived in Romania. We've had up to a hundred contractors on site since the house was positioned, to get the renovations done. They only finished planting up the borders under floodlights last night.'

'But I hadn't even paid for the land.'

'Keith sorted it. Along with Maggie and me. She's quite some woman, your aunt, isn't she?'

'You've been *talking* to Maggie?'

'I wanted to talk to you but Maggie didn't think you were ready to listen at first. And then she came up with the idea of surprising you. Showing you that you hadn't lost as much as you thought you had.'

'Including you?'

'Especially me.' Nic kissed her again and his breath came out in a sigh that sounded like relief. 'That was why I agreed to the plan to keep it a secret. I had to know I could pull this together because I didn't want to promise something I couldn't deliver. I don't want you to ever again doubt that you can trust me.'

'I don't. I didn't… I was confused, that was all. There

were too many things happening all at once and they were too big… I couldn't take it in fast enough.'

She looked around her again. 'I still can't take *this* in. Whose idea were the nasturtiums?'

'Mine.' Nic was smiling again. 'They're the colour of flames and they make me think of you.'

'Oh, Nic… You have no idea how much I love you.'

'I don't know about that.' Nic bent to kiss her yet again. 'But I hope it's at least half as much as I love you.' When he lifted his mouth he touched his forehead to hers for a long, solemn moment.

'Je t'adore, ma chérie.'

She needed no translation. 'I love you, too,' she whispered back.

With her hand held within the circle of his fingers, Nic led Zanna inside. He had poured his heart and soul into this project for weeks and he'd never been so tired. Or so nervous about the result. Had he done justice to the home she had lived in for most of her life and loved so much? Changes had had to be made but that was life, wasn't it? You let go of some things and that meant you could choose the best and treasure them.

The interior walls of the house had been relined and painted in soft, pastel shades of lemon and cream. New carpets had been laid but the design and colours fitted the period of the house perfectly. New curtains graced windows with wooden framing that glowed richly after the timber had been stripped and restored.

'It feels so different,' Zanna murmured. 'So *light*…'

'It's not hemmed in by high-rise buildings any more. We've positioned it so it will get maximum sunlight, even in the winter.'

'You got everything out of storage. You've even put

the antique instruments back in the same places. And Maggie's hats… Oh, I'm glad we put them into storage before the fire. They wouldn't have survived the smoke.'

The beams in the room that had been Spellbound were the only reminder of the fire. They had been cleaned and polished but would always be misshapen and stained.

'Because you can't wipe out the past,' Nic said softly. 'And sometimes you have to honour it because it's what has made you what you are today.'

Every new surprise was a delight. Her bedroom with the painting she had done of Nic playing the guitar hanging over the head of the bed they had shared. The flowered walls intact and the blooms as bright as when they'd first been painted.

'We got lucky and found an electrician with a bit of imagination. He found places for the new plugs without having to ruin a single flower. And a plumber who looked after the ivy in the bathroom.'

Even the tiled floor in the kitchen had been saved and relaid. A new courtyard of recycled bricks lay beyond the French doors with the chiminea set amongst a collection of terracotta pots. The old rustic table and chairs were waiting. A bottle of champagne stood in an ice bucket with two stemmed glasses in invitation.

But Zanna didn't see them. Her hand gripped Nic's hard enough to cut off the circulation in his fingers as she stared at the terracotta pots filled with flame-coloured geraniums. To where there were three black shapes emerging from between the pots and coming towards her.

Letting go of Nic's hand, Zanna dropped to a crouch and gathered the wash of black fur into her arms. Tears of joy were on her cheeks as she looked up at him.

'They're alive...' she whispered.

'I found them the day we were lifting the house. Or Merlin found me.'

'He's a clever cat. He knew you were special right from the moment he met you.' Zanna was on her feet again. 'Like I did.'

He took her into his arms again. He never wanted to let her go.

'Is it all right? Is it how you imagined it could be?'

'Better. Unbelievable. I still have no idea how you could possibly have pulled this off.' Zanna's smile was misty. 'I know I really do believe in magic now.' She pulled away far enough to catch Nic's gaze. 'But I don't want to live here.'

His jaw dropped. Time stopped.

'Alone,' Zanna added. 'I couldn't live here without you, Nic. This place is perfect but...it's a house and—'

'And home is where the heart is,' Nic finished for her.

Her nod was solemn. 'Mine is with you,' she said. 'For ever.'

It was too hard to find words. Too big. All Nic could do was tilt his head in a single nod to signal his agreement. To kiss this woman he loved so much in a way that would let her know he felt exactly the same way.

For ever was going to start right now.

EPILOGUE

A year later...

THE SPEECHES WERE over and the crowd poised to applaud.

Nic's hand covered Zanna's so that they were both holding the oversized ceremonial scissors they were using to cut the wide scarlet ribbon.

The Brabant Music Academy was officially open.

The beautiful, curved building that echoed the flow of the river was being hailed as one of the most significant new assets of the city. The acoustic masterpiece of a concert hall would cater for the most discerning musicians and their fans. The numerous, soundproofed tutorial rooms would give the students what they needed to be nurtured into the futures they dreamed of. The later addition of the café and courtyard garden would encourage others to step into a world they might not otherwise have entered and the space tagged for after-school and holiday programmes might inspire members of a new generation.

Members of the symphony orchestra were playing in the concert hall as the invited guests toured the academy. Herbal tea, champagne and organic canapés were available in the café.

Nic was still holding Zanna's hand as they mingled and talked to people. So far, they hadn't made it past the foyer that housed the gallery of beautiful black and white photographs of Rata House—the captions below sharing the history of the land on which the school now stood. One of the images was in colour. And it was a painting rather than a photograph. A scene of the house reborn, with the lake in the foreground and the back-drop of the native bush.

'This is one of your paintings, Zanna?' The mayor looked impressed. 'I must get to your next exhibition. I'm told your first was a sell-out.'

'Of course it was.' The pride in Nic's voice was matched by the loving glance between the couple.

The mayor continued to admire the painting. 'It looks like it was always meant to be there. I'm delighted to see that someone had the vision to preserve such a special part of our city's heritage. And in such spectacular fash-ion. I suspect you're a bit of a magician, Nic.'

'No magic involved. Just a dream and a lot of hard work.'

'I'll bet. You deserve the privilege of having it as your home.'

'One of our homes.' Zanna smiled. 'We intend to spend half our year in France, where we have another house.'

'Ah...' The mayor nodded. 'I heard that was where you went to get married?'

'No,' Zanna laughed. 'We got married in a castle. In Transylvania. Let me introduce you to my aunt Magda and her husband. They've come all the way from Ro-mania for this opening ceremony.'

Maggie was delighted to meet the mayor. 'I can't tell you what a lovely surprise it was to find the council has planted rata trees on the avenue. Such lovely, big specimens, too.'

'Mr Brabant got the biggest one available. Have you seen it out there on the lawn?'

'We're heading that way now.' Zanna linked her arm with Maggie's and smiled at Dimitry. 'Let's go and find you both a glass of something bubbly so we can celebrate properly.'

There was so much to celebrate but Zanna wouldn't be drinking anything more than a cup of herbal tea. She met Maggie's gaze over the rim of her cup a short time later.

'So the cards were right.' Her aunt smiled. 'I had a feeling the Empress was there for more than the birth of a creative child.'

It was too early for it to be any more than a guess but there was no point in trying to keep it a secret.

'We only just found out.'

'Congratulations.' Dimitry's eyes looked suspiciously moist. 'Such happy news.'

'I think it will be a girl,' Maggie pronounced.

Zanna looked up at Nic. 'If it is,' she said softly, 'I'd like to name her Elise.'

He had to take her away then. To a quiet spot away from the crowd. To the bench seat that had been placed on the river side of the rata tree on the lawn. The seat with the small brass plaque that carried his parents' names.

So that he could kiss his wife and tell her again just how much he loved her.

So that he could hear her tell him the same thing.

He'd been wrong in telling the mayor that no magic had been involved. And hadn't he told Zanna within the first few minutes of meeting her that he wouldn't believe in magic in a million years?

Well…he had just changed his mind. It was the only word to describe this—the alchemy of finding the person you wanted to be with for ever that only happened when they felt exactly the same way.

There was more magic to be found as well. Very strong magic that meant this was one spell that would never be broken.

Ever.

* * * * *

Mills & Boon® Hardback

September 2014

ROMANCE

The Housekeeper's Awakening	Sharon Kendrick
More Precious than a Crown	Carol Marinelli
Captured by the Sheikh	Kate Hewitt
A Night in the Prince's Bed	Chantelle Shaw
Damaso Claims His Heir	Annie West
Changing Constantinou's Game	Jennifer Hayward
The Ultimate Revenge	Victoria Parker
Tycoon's Temptation	Trish Morey
The Party Dare	Anne Oliver
Sleeping with the Soldier	Charlotte Phillips
All's Fair in Lust & War	Amber Page
Dressed to Thrill	Bella Frances
Interview with a Tycoon	Cara Colter
Her Boss by Arrangement	Teresa Carpenter
In Her Rival's Arms	Alison Roberts
Frozen Heart, Melting Kiss	Ellie Darkins
After One Forbidden Night...	Amber McKenzie
Dr Perfect on Her Doorstep	Lucy Clark

MEDICAL

A Secret Shared...	Marion Lennox
Flirting with the Doc of Her Dreams	Janice Lynn
The Doctor Who Made Her Love Again	Susan Carlisle
The Maverick Who Ruled Her Heart	Susan Carlisle

ROMANCE

The Only Woman to Defy Him	Carol Marinelli
Secrets of a Ruthless Tycoon	Cathy Williams
Gambling with the Crown	Lynn Raye Harris
The Forbidden Touch of Sanguardo	Julia James
One Night to Risk it All	Maisey Yates
A Clash with Cannavaro	Elizabeth Power
The Truth About De Campo	Jennifer Hayward
Expecting the Prince's Baby	Rebecca Winters
The Millionaire's Homecoming	Cara Colter
The Heir of the Castle	Scarlet Wilson
Twelve Hours of Temptation	Shoma Narayanan

HISTORICAL

Unwed and Unrepentant	Marguerite Kaye
Return of the Prodigal Gilvry	Ann Lethbridge
A Traitor's Touch	Helen Dickson
Yield to the Highlander	Terri Brisbin
Return of the Viking Warrior	Michelle Styles

MEDICAL

Waves of Temptation	Marion Lennox
Risk of a Lifetime	Caroline Anderson
To Play with Fire	Tina Beckett
The Dangers of Dating Dr Carvalho	Tina Beckett
Uncovering Her Secrets	Amalie Berlin
Unlocking the Doctor's Heart	Susanne Hampton

Mills & Boon® Hardback

October 2014

ROMANCE

An Heiress for His Empire	Lucy Monroe
His for a Price	Caitlin Crews
Commanded by the Sheikh	Kate Hewitt
The Valquez Bride	Melanie Milburne
The Uncompromising Italian	Cathy Williams
Prince Hafiz's Only Vice	Susanna Carr
A Deal Before the Altar	Rachael Thomas
Rival's Challenge	Abby Green
The Party Starts at Midnight	Lucy King
Your Bed or Mine?	Joss Wood
Turning the Good Girl Bad	Avril Tremayne
Breaking the Bro Code	Stefanie London
The Billionaire in Disguise	Soraya Lane
The Unexpected Honeymoon	Barbara Wallace
A Princess by Christmas	Jennifer Faye
His Reluctant Cinderella	Jessica Gilmore
One More Night with Her Desert Prince...	Jennifer Taylor
From Fling to Forever	Avril Tremayne

MEDICAL

It Started with No Strings...	Kate Hardy
Flirting with Dr Off-Limits	Robin Gianna
Dare She Date Again?	Amy Ruttan
The Surgeon's Christmas Wish	Annie O'Neil

0914GEN STD HB

ROMANCE

Ravelli's Defiant Bride	Lynne Graham
When Da Silva Breaks the Rules	Abby Green
The Heartbreaker Prince	Kim Lawrence
The Man She Can't Forget	Maggie Cox
A Question of Honour	Kate Walker
What the Greek Can't Resist	Maya Blake
An Heir to Bind Them	Dani Collins
Becoming the Prince's Wife	Rebecca Winters
Nine Months to Change His Life	Marion Lennox
Taming Her Italian Boss	Fiona Harper
Summer with the Millionaire	Jessica Gilmore

HISTORICAL

Scars of Betrayal	Sophia James
Scandal's Virgin	Louise Allen
An Ideal Companion	Anne Ashley
Surrender to the Viking	Joanna Fulford
No Place for an Angel	Gail Whitiker

MEDICAL

200 Harley Street: Surgeon in a Tux	Carol Marinelli
200 Harley Street: Girl from the Red Carpet	Scarlet Wilson
Flirting with the Socialite Doc	Melanie Milburne
His Diamond Like No Other	Lucy Clark
The Last Temptation of Dr Dalton	Robin Gianna
Resisting Her Rebel Hero	Lucy Ryder